BESSIE HEAD, one of Africa's best-known women writers, was born in South Africa in 1937, the result of an 'illicit' union between a black man and a white woman. Her life was a traumatic one, and she drew heavily upon her own experiences for her novels. She was looked after by a foster family until she was thirteen, and then attended a mission school. She trained as a teacher. After four years' teaching she took a job as a journalist for *Drum* magazine, but an unsuccessful marriage and her involvement in the trial of a friend led her to apply for a teaching post in Botswana, where she took up permanent exile. Her precarious refugee status lasted fifteen years until she was granted Botswana citizenship in 1979.

Botswana is the backdrop for all three of her novels. *When Rain Clouds Gather*, her first novel, based on her time as a refugee living at the Bamangwato Development Farm, was published in 1969. This was followed by *Maru* (1971) and the intense and powerful autobiographical work *A Question of Power* (1974). Her short stories appeared as *The Collector of Treasures* in 1977, and in 1981 *Serowe: Village of the Rain Wind* was published, a historical portrait of a hundred years of a community in Botswana.

Bessie Head died in 1986, aged 49. *A Woman Alone*, a collection of autobiographical writings, *Tales of Tenderness and Power* and *The Cardinals* were published posthumously.

BESSIE HEAD

THE CARDINALS

With Meditations and Short Stories

Edited by M. J. Daymond

Heinemann

Heinemann Educational Publishers
Halley Court, Jordan Hill, Oxford OX2 8EJ
a division of Reed Educational & Professional Publishing Ltd

Heinemann: A Division of Reed Publishing (USA) Inc.
361 Hanover Street, Portsmouth, NH 03801-3912, USA

Heinemann Educational Books (Nigeria) Ltd
PMB 5205, Ibadan

Heinemann Educational Boleswa
PO Box 10103, Village Post Office, Gaborone, Botswana

MELBOURNE   AUCKLAND
FLORENCE   PRAGUE   MADRID   ATHENS
SINGAPORE   TOKYO   SAO PAULO
CHICAGO   PORTSMOUTH (NH)   MEXICO
IBADAN   GABORONE   JOHANNESBURG
KAMPALA   NAIROBI

First published in Southern Africa by David Philip Publishers (Pty) Ltd.
1993
First published by Heinemann Educational Publishers in 1995

British Library Cataloguing in Publication Data
A catalogue record for this book is available from the British Library.

ISBN 0 435 90967 3

Series Editors:
Chinua Achebe 1962–1990
Adewale Maja-Pearce 1990–94

Series Consultant Abdulrazak Gurnah 1994

Cover design by *Touchpaper*
Cover illustration by Alan Bond
Author photograph by George Hallett

Printed and bound in Great Britain by
Cox & Wyman Ltd, Reading, Berkshire

97 98 99 8 7 6 5 4 3 2

Contents

Introduction

The Cardinals is probably the first long piece of fiction that Bessie Head produced and it is the only one that she set in South Africa. Written while she was in Cape Town, 1960–62, it was not published during her life-time. The manuscript was certainly sent to publishers, possibly in England as well as in South Africa, but no one accepted it. When she left South Africa for Serowe in 1964, or shortly after she arrived in Botswana, Bessie Head made a present of the typescript to Patrick Cullinan. He had been helping her financially and also, as she had been refused a passport, in the business of getting the one-way exit permit on which she had to leave the country of her birth for ever. It was all she had to give. Her letters to him,[1] and those published by Randolph Vigne,[2] indicate that the meditations and short stories which are also published here for the first time were among the many pieces she sent to Patrick Cullinan during her first months in Botswana. The arrangement was that he would have them typed so that she could submit her work to international magazines which might publish and pay for it. He handled this task for her in South Africa.

Bessie Head was desperately poor. When the teaching job she had taken up in Serowe came to a sudden end, she had no means of supporting herself and her young child, Howard. Writing seemed to be her only possible source of income until she could acquire other skills useful to her new country – she wanted to study agriculture. Although she spent some months at a development farm near Palapye (about 50 kilometres from Serowe), it proved impossible to get the scholarship she needed and so she had to battle on from day to day, writing as and when she could. It took several hard years before recognition came, for, although eight stories and essays appeared in the interim, as well as reviews commissioned for *The*

New African, it was not until 1966, when *The New Statesman* published a sketch called 'The Woman from America', that interest in her was kindled. A commission from the American publishers, Simon & Schuster, followed and *When Rain Clouds Gather*, which has until now been thought of as Bessie Head's first long fiction, appeared in 1968.

That Bessie Head had always felt herself to be a writer is clear from *The Cardinals*, which is a passionate exploration of the craft and the calling. For two years before writing it, she had been working as a journalist for the weekly supplement of the Johannesburg *Golden City Post*, writing columns for teenagers and children, and helping Dolly Hassim to produce the escapist love stories that were a counterpoint to the paper's a-political sensationalism and muck-raking. Writing as 'Aunt Bessie' for her young readers, she broke abruptly with the column's earlier assumption that its teenage readers were moody, self-centred, love-lorn 'kids' and worked hard to turn their interests outward, to the actual world around them. In keeping with her efforts to redirect her young readers' interests, *The Cardinals* suggests that the radiance of ordinary daily life was what she wanted to capture in her own writing. The discrepancy between the inner stability from which such a vision had to spring and the hate-filled legislation, such as the Immorality Act, with which the Nationalist Government was then entrenching apartheid, seems however to have been too great for her to contain. This legislation, which progressively outlawed sexual union between black and white people, has a long history. In 1927, the first country-wide prohibition on sexual union between white and African people outside of marriage was passed; in 1950 this prohibition was extended to include Indian and 'coloured' people. In 1957 the amendments which are referred to in *The Cardinals* were passed. In them, most behaviour of a sexual nature involving white and black people was criminalised – imprisonment of up to 7 years could follow from just inviting a person of another race to perform the illicit sexual act. The legislation was effective in the sense that the young sailor whose trial Mouse has to cover would have been one of 6 000 people convicted under its provisions between 1950 and 1966. But, as the further amendments of 1967 and 1969 suggest, laws such as this could not prevent all racial contact of a sexual nature.[3]

Given such legislation, which was bolstered by numerous other laws, it is only too clear why, shortly after arriving in Serowe, Bessie Head wrote to Patrick Cullinan that she felt South Africa to be 'a place that crushes dreams'. While she was in the country her responses to political oppression were intense, but, as she explained later, what drove her out of South Africa was not so much the consequences of her own political activity as the impossibility of writing in a land whose laws enacted fear and hatred.

On these grounds alone, Bessie Head had ample reason to fear the task of writing in South Africa. So much that was ugly and destructive in the world around her demanded to be recorded. In addition, she seems to have feared herself as a writer, to have battled against the fear that the cruelty and deprivation she had suffered as a rejected child might have marked her inwardly too. In *A Question of Power*, the novel published in 1973, she records both the misery, the unnameable terrors, of being a rejected child of unknown parents and the fear that this experience had made her a collaborator with evil, one who would create suffering wherever she went. The view, that she believed was held by the family which had denied her, that her mother's associating with (and having a child by) a black man was enough to brand her insane, was thrust on Bessie Head when she was about twelve years old; what she never knew was the identity of her father. What we can now see in *The Cardinals* is how, from the beginning, she worked to transmute this personal pain and fear into larger, impersonal forms of expression. She strove to make space in the material which came to her from her own life for what she saw and understood from other lives around her.

Much of the energy of her writing comes from the conflicts she knew. Her passionate belief in the potential beauty of life collided with the ugliness she had been subjected to as a child and which she saw every day around her as an adult. These collisions are always stark and elemental, and they take on metaphysical dimensions; ugliness threatens beauty, the forces of good confront those of evil. Bessie Head's interest in how such collisions might arise in an individual life is evident from the first protagonist she created – the young woman whom we meet as Miriam, as Charlotte and finally as Mouse: 'a beautiful soul that was nurtured on a dung heap'.

That Bessie Head did not think poverty produced only ugliness or that writing was necessarily to be feared is evident in the wonderful opening scenes of *The Cardinals* in which the world of the child, Miriam, opens before her eyes as she discovers the thrill of reading and of writing. She does it through an old man and a book that she retrieves from a rubbish heap. Learning to write her name gives her a hold on her identity; what it cannot give her is the power, or the confidence, to give this identity to others. She is too shut off to do it in her daily life, nor can she do it in writing. What begins the process of closing her off is her encounter with the prohibited face of sexuality – she flees from the drunken advances of her foster father. For her release, she has to be bullied and lured out of the state of frozen fear into which she has retreated. And sexual passion is again what will do this. The person who can bring it about is Johnny, the intense, cynical idealist and dreamer whom she meets on the newspaper, *The African Beat*. But he is not only a fellow journalist; he is, unknown to either of them, also her father.

To begin to understand why Bessie Head might have written a taboo into her protagonist's fulfilment as a writer and as a woman, we have to go again to her society as well as to her own life. And this way we can also begin to see why it was the Immorality Act, of all the many laws which sought to entrench white power in South Africa by keeping the races apart, which so angered Bessie Head. Its provisions must have brought about the fusion of personal fears and political angers which is evident in *The Cardinals*. The individual rejection that Bessie Head had suffered as a child (of all her family, only her white grandmother had visited her in the orphanage – and that only once) was now being matched by the annihilating rejection of a whole people that was implicit in the legislation. Its prohibitions were sexual, so that the very union which had produced her was now a criminal act; but they were also existential, so that people like Bessie Head must have felt that their right to exist was being called into question. The attitude that she was confronting is clear in a speech in parliament

on the Population Registration Act, which enforced the racial classifi-
cation of all South Africans, made by the Minister of the Interior. In
it he said that the intention was 'to close the gate so we cannot
continue indefinitely creating new borderline cases as rapidly as we
deal with the already existing cases.'⁴ As a 'case' herself, Bessie Head
had much to protest.

She was not, however, one for simple protest-writing; as she put it
in a letter to Patrick Cullinan that was written from Serowe but before
she had begun to find her subject matter in Botswana:

> It's no longer South Africa and protest writing. It's myself and
> myself alone that I have to present. A protest is an excuse, a
> cover up. I no longer have that and besides it's the lowest form
> of writing. Anyone can be justifiably indignant.

If she did not respect a writing of the surfaces of anger, she also
understood the dangers of taking political anger into herself so that it
fused with other aspects of her being. In another letter she wrote:

> I don't think you know what it is to awaken every morning to
> a burning hatred against injustice. It isn't an abstract thing, you
> are hating people and the perpetrators of this injustice. You
> come eventually to the conclusion that both the hater and the
> hated will blow up in a great conflagration.

And she said, in a letter written in 1982, that she 'shuddered with
horror' when she re-read a forgotten poem, called 'Things I Don't
Like', which she had written after the massacre in Sharpeville in 1960,
because it 'advocates indiscriminate violence and bloodshed'.

In *The Cardinals* she did, however, take the risk of writing her
profoundest angers in non-protest form. A sense of what she was
risking as well as the anger she felt can be seen in her choice of an
almost forbidden subject, incest, for her novella. The unwittingly
incestuous love which grows between Mouse and Johnny can be read
as dramatising and defining her political anger – when set against the
trivialising, power-serving prohibitions of the Immorality Act, the

taboo on incest is a serious matter. The forbidden nature of such love also dramatises the fear Bessie Head must have felt at releasing into her writing the angers which stemmed from her own early suffering.

For all the barriers that she had to break in writing this novella, and although no triumph (neither the consummation nor the writing that the love will release) is put before us, Bessie Head does make us believe that her protagonists have the right to love each other. And through our sympathy for the lovers' particular plight, we are encouraged to read expansively so that their ignorance of their blood ties comes to speak in general terms of the risks involved in any passionate venture – in writing itself. To provide such links would have been an extraordinary achievement for any novelist; here it is done by a young woman of about twenty-five writing her first long work of fiction.

At one level, the love plot of *The Cardinals* rests on a cliché handsome, worldly man meets and loves shrinking violet. This was the basis of many of the escapist romances Bessie Head had handled each week at *Golden City Post*: they were fodder offered in compensation for the subjection that women suffered. But, more profoundly, the germ of Bessie Head's story lies in folk tale, in the ancient story of the maiden princess imprisoned in a tower awaiting her prince and rescue. As the story of Mouse and Johnny, it speaks more deeply to us than the clichés of romance ever could. Its retelling in the story of Johnny and Ruby, Mouse's unknown mother, is a reminder that not every woman has the courage to take up the freedom that love offers. When Mouse turns Johnny's early life into a short story, depicting his first discovery that sex and death are adjacent, the courage demanded by her imaginative recognitions tells us why Mouse qualifies as a princess. She might also be a writer.

The Cardinals is not only expressive of complex fears and angers. There is a haunting beauty in its many love stories; there is a real pathos in a waif's searching for a wheel-chair that will never reach the old lady who needs it; there is an unerring eye for the pretensions of sexual combat; there are glimpses of what it means to find in jazz an echo and a challenge to one's own suffering; there are the exchanges in the fish-and-chips shop to tell us that District Six (the slum in Cape Town where Bessie Head and her characters lived and which was proclaimed a 'whites only' area in 1966) was a polyglot little world. The glimpses we get of the spirited exchanges of daily life combine with the descriptions of Johnny's house to remind us that had Bessie Head been able to continue writing in South Africa, she could have written of life on the other side of privilege in ways that South African writers and readers, having been denied what she promised thirty years ago, are only now beginning to find. And there are several indications that Bessie Head knew what she had to offer. The final task that we see Johnny giving Mouse is for her to capture, in drawing and then in words, something of the meaning of the natural and the man-made world around her – she has to articulate the understanding that sitting high on the mountain can give her of the city beneath. Whether or not she succeeds is an open question. But what the exercise does tell us is that Bessie Head herself knew how important it was for a writer to find a meeting point between the world around her and what she had to offer from within.

It is the ground-work for such a living contact with her new world in Serowe that we find Bessie Head beginning to undertake in the first pieces of writing that she sent to Patrick Cullinan from Botswana. As we have seen, she was fully aware of the stage she had reached in the task before her: 'It's no longer South Africa and protest writing. It's myself and myself alone that I have to present.' She was looking for ways of giving form to the beauty she believed in, and which she trusted her new world would offer. Thus in the first two of the meditations published here, 'Earth and Everything' and 'Africa', Bessie Head, writing in response to the physical beauty around her, imagines a man who is its equal and the love that such a person would warrant. The resultant writing speaks of the isolation which caused her to reach deep into herself, and of its leading to the analogical thinking on which allegorical writing is based. But, although she loosens it, she does not lose her grasp on actuality in these pieces. Her feeling for the physical world fuses with her idealism in passages like this, from 'Where is the Hour of the Beautiful Dancing of Birds in the Sun-wind?':

*the man I love is all men. Always I was a part of all life, but
only now in a meaningful sense, so that the rain-wind and sun-
wind of Africa beat about my face, arms, legs and the earth-pull
is strong in my body which is vividly, intensely alive.*

It was not for nothing that Bessie Head admired D. H. Lawrence
and that like him she wanted, as she said in a letter to Patrick
Cullinan, to have her 'footsteps . . . hitting the earth.'

That she also had not lost her commonsense while creating such
flights of fancy is evident in another remark in one of her letters of
this time. Writing of South Africa, she observed:

*Afrikaners love that country possessively and it's with a
destructive kind of love that wants to crush and keep the loved
thing all to itself. A land and a people can form that kind of
affinity – just like a love between a man and a woman. It's
wonderful to love but, God knows, it must be tempered with a
little bit of sanity. The whole world should not come to a full
stop because someone loves something or someone!*

Although the uncertainties and trials of her life seem to have upset
her balance at times, and to have made her irascible and difficult,
there is a humour in such writing which indicates the kind of courage
with which she faced her exile. It appears again in 'A Personal View
of the Survival of the Unfittest' when she writes in praise of her
backbone: 'There is nothing pessimistic or neurotic about a backbone.
It is the jauntiest, gayest thing in the world, forever driving the body,
mind and soul forward in this ceaseless urge to live, live, live.'

Although Bessie Head never learned more than a smattering of any
of the languages of Botswana, she clearly had a good ear for a tale in
speech. As she says of the testimony on which she based 'Poor Man',
'The poetic expression and deep sorrow – everything – is Mr
Magane's'. This ability to hear the poetry of others is like her ability
to see into the beauty of the land and, in some respects, the way of
life around her. All of the qualities that Bessie Head brought with her
to Botswana, and all of the beauties she was learning to see around

her meet in the tale 'Earth Love'. In a letter of this period, Bessie Head indicated that perhaps its title should be changed to 'The Jackal Blanket Maker' (Vigne, p.23), but in this context, in which we can trace her gradual discovery of what her new country could offer her as a writer, her original title seems more appropriate. She herself thought of it as 'the most goddam best bit of writing I ever did' (Vigne, p.23).

Bessie Head was a good judge of her own writing. She could stand back from what she was attempting, looking at it quizzically as often as affectionately. The man she created in Johnny clearly puzzled her even as he pleased her. In her only comment on *The Cardinals* that has so far surfaced, she wrote to Patrick Cullinan:

> *You know – that funny book I sent – 'The Cardinals' – I started to create a mythical man there and he has since appeared everywhere. I write about him all the time – yet he is not a flesh and blood reality. But everytime I need to say something about love – he's always there – so conveniently. Don't you think he'd be rather over-used? He gets better and better with each story but how can one write about a non-existent person? I can't understand this phenomenon. We exchange words too. Sometimes he talks in his intense way and sometimes I do all the talking. I can't understand it but that's just how it is. I'm just worried that I won't be able to understand a real man or else I'll get caught out one day. He is the 'Green Tree'. He is 'Africa' and the 'Beautiful Birds Dancing in the Sun-wind,' and 'Earth and Everything.' One day it's going to back-fire. I know it. Imagination is somethingI distrust profoundly and the way I have created this man out of air, shocks me in a terrible way, in my reasonable moments.*

Perhaps she was right to wonder about her creation. And perhaps she was right about Johnny's getting 'better and better with each story'. Certainly in *Maru*, Bessie Head does more with him than anything she attempts in the work published here. But then, the Johnny of *The Cardinals* has something unique, something that was never to appear again in Bessie Head's writing. He is decidedly unmythical in that his District Six origins come through all the time – he is at once sharp and funny and angry. He should have the last word about himself as he speaks to his colleague, James, about his writing:

> *Your writing bores me to death. Every single story I've read of yours is about the happy little Coloured man and the colourful Malays. Why don't you leave that crap to those insane, patronising White women journalists who are forever at pains to tell the Coloureds how happy they are. Why don't you stay a dead-end kid and like it? It's a great life!*

Johnny might be speaking scornfully, but *The Cardinals* also gives us the truth of what he says. He likes his identity. He and Mouse may be doomed or they may triumph, but whichever way it goes for individual readers, they have been given by their writer a power to make and to question their lives which no laws could finally gainsay.

M. J. Daymond

Permission to quote from the unpublished letters has been kindly given by the Bessie Head archive in the Khama III Memorial Museum, Serowe.
1. These letters will be published by David Philip in 1994.
2. *A Sense of Belonging*, published by Heinemann Educational Books and by S A Writers, London, in 1991. Quotations from this collection are identified by 'Vigne' and a page reference.
3. This information is taken from an article by Ellison Kahn in *The Standard Encyclopaedia of Southern Africa*, vol 6, 1972, and from Brian Bunting's *The Rise of the Third Reich*, 1986.
4. Quoted in Bunting, p. 160.

The Cardinals

The Cardinals, in the astrological sense, are those who serve as the base or foundation for change.

1

It was a large slum area of tin shacks, bounded on the one side by a mile-long graveyard and on the other by the city refuse dump and the sea. A national road separated the slum from the refuse dump.

On a day in June 1937 a car stopped alongside on the road and a beautiful young woman climbed out with a wrapped-up bundle in her arms. She wrinkled her nose in distaste as the stench of the refuse dump and the slum assaulted it; then, holding her breath at intervals, she picked her way carefully through the sand, night-soil and stagnant water between the shack houses. Thin dogs tied to the shack houses barked hysterically as she passed, causing the shack dwellers to come out of their dark and smoky hovels and peer at her curiously.

She knocked on one of the makeshift doors and a woman inside tugged it open. The hot, stifling air of the interior of the shack struck the young woman full in the face and she steeled herself to enter. It was a small space with every possible bit of junk crammed into it; boxes stuffed with rags and faded clothing; an old, cracked mirror in a corner; a torn, stained mattress competing for space with battered pots, an oil stove, blankets and a small, shaky, wooden table.

'Hello, Sarah,' said the young woman with a forced brightness. 'I've brought the baby.'

The woman Sarah said nothing. She took the bundle that was handed towards her. The young woman opened her purse and placed five shillings on the wooden table, then, without another look at the bundle in the arms of the other woman, turned and walked swiftly out of the shack towards the waiting car.

The neighbours were curious but guarded about showing it. Living in such close proximity to each other, they tried to keep up a pretence of each man's minding his own business knowing full well that what little entertainment they squeezed out of life was in exchanging gossip about each other.

A friend of the woman Sarah who lived in the next shack could contain herself no longer and went over to find out what had caused the visit of the young woman. She pushed open the door and saw Sarah sitting on an upturned box with the bundle in her arms.

'What have you here, my sister?' she asked.

'A child,' said Sarah.

Her friend nodded knowingly. 'It belongs to the young woman?'

'Yes.'

'What is it doing here with you then?'

'She has given it to me.'

Sarah indicated the five shillings on the table. Her friend snorted in contempt: 'That is not much. You should have asked for more. What kind of woman is it who will sell her child for five shillings?'

'It is not so, Lena. I agreed to take the child without asking for money. The young lady is well known to me as I do the washing at her home. She is to marry soon. This child was an accident from another man. The one she is to marry has said that he will not have the child. The family approached me and I agreed to take the little one as my own.'

'What does your man say to this?'

'He is agreeable too. We have none of our own as you know.'

Her friend snorted again. 'I think you are a fool to take another man's accident. Should the authorities get to know of this you will be in trouble.'

The woman Sarah opened the bundle on her lap and the two women examined it.

'A girl,' said her friend pessimistically. 'It is always more trouble to rear a girl.'

'But it is a pretty child,' the woman Sarah said tenderly. 'Look, it has opened its eyes. They are like great round moons and as black as the night when the moon does not shine. Have you seen such eyes on a child before?'

Her friend admired the baby grudgingly. 'I still say you are a fool. It is always hard to find food for an extra mouth.'

Sarah smiled and said nothing. She knew it was only womanly envy that make her friend talk that way.

'What have you thought to name her?' Lena asked.

'Miriam,' she said.

◆

Until the age of ten, that was the only world the child knew. Early each morning the men crept out of the tin shacks to work as labourers in the town. Those women who had no work sat around idly and gossiped. The children had to walk a mile from the slum with pails or tins to collect water for household use, then they would spend the rest of the day raking around in the refuse dump for edibles or discarded clothing or any other treasure. During weekdays life was quiet. On Friday evenings when the men received their pay, the night would be a riot of violence and drunkenness.

The protectiveness and love of the woman Sarah secluded her from much of the crudeness and harshness of the life. Her quiet and solemn reserve protected her further. She was the type of child who preferred to be alone.

One day a jolly old man with a twinkle in his eye made his appearance in the slum and straightaway set up a makeshift house of tin, cardboard and sacking, under the big tree that stood near the edge of the slum. He announced himself as a tobacco-seller, but, when it was discovered that he could read and write, his prestige soared high. He was often requested to write a letter and the fact that the old man copied out stock letters from a book entitled *The Art of Letter Writing* did not seem strange or amusing to anyone. The book could handle all the problems of life which required a letter. In a community that could neither read nor write his services were much valued. He always received a remuneration for every letter he wrote. The old man spent all the money he earned on food and drink. When drunk, he had an annoying habit of singing for hours on end in a high-pitched voice but the people of the slum merely laughed indulgently.

'Just listen to the old man,' they said, shaking their heads and laughing. Usually such a display of individualism would have been violently repressed but the valuable service he performed for the community set him apart and protected him. The way his hands and body continuously trembled from age and dissipated living also warmed and softened their blind, brutal hearts and made them want to protect him.

The old man became accustomed to the silent and solemn-eyed child who stood at a distance watching him with a fascinated interest. An acknowledged but unspoken friendship developed between them. It was only her shyness and reserve that prevented her from approaching too closely. If she noticed him looking at her she would walk away quietly, swinging a stick at the ground. But the day came when she could contain her curiosity no longer.

'What are you doing, Uncle?' she asked.

He looked up with a friendly twinkle in his eye. 'I am writing a letter,' he said.

'What is a letter?' she asked.

'A letter has many uses,' he said. 'It is to give news of a new arrival in the world. It is to express grief at the death of an old friend. It is for a young man to propose to a young lady.'

She pointed to the letter he was writing with an explicit question in her eyes.

'This is a letter to express grief,' he said.

'What does it say, Uncle?' she asked.

He read the letter to her:

> *My dear Jonathan,*
> *It is with great sorrow that I learnt the news of the death of your beloved father. He was a great and worthy man. I and the family send condolence to you in your hour of loss and grief.*
> *Your devoted friend,*
> *Elijah.*

She pointed to the book and the writing pad with a question in her eyes. It sent the old man into a fit of laughter. When he could talk he said admiringly: 'You are a clever child. No one here questions why I should use the book to write a letter. Should another man come and ask me to write a condolence I would write this same letter.'

The child smiled solemnly.

'Have you been to school yet, little one?' he asked. She shook her head.

'It is a pity,' he said, sadly. 'You would learn fast. You have a questioning mind. I did not go to school also. I had to teach myself'

She stretched out a finger and touched the printed words on the book then pointed to the refuse dump.

'I see a lot of this over there,' she said.

'You must bring it to me, little one,' he said with his twinkling smile.

She pointed to his handwriting on the pad.

'Can I do this too?' she asked.

'Yes,' he said.

'Show me.'

'I will teach you to write your name. Tell me what it is.'

She told him. He removed a sheet of paper and, with a shaky hand in bold print, wrote MIRIAM. He showed her how to hold the pencil and guided her hand to trace over the letters. After a few tracings she became excited and clutched the paper to her chest. He gave her the writing pad and she ran behind the tree. She traced the letters over several times then tried to write her version. For some odd reason everything turned out the wrong way round. She squinted hard at the two versions and tried again. The same thing happened. She was busy a long time and the old man had begun to doze when she suddenly burst on him with a triumphant, radiant face.

'Look, Uncle!' At the bottom of the page was an almost perfect reproduction of her name the way he had printed it.

From that day she learnt to write rapidly. The old man was amazed at this display of seriousness and purpose in such a small child. He praised her lavishly and untiringly. Soon she was able to copy out a letter from the book of letter writing.

One day, while standing knee-deep in the dirt of the refuse dump, she found a brightly illustrated picture book and sped off with it to the old man.

'What's this, Uncle?' she asked, trembling with excitement.

The old man took it eagerly in his shaking hands and read out slowly: '*The Adventures of Fuzzy Wuzzy Bear*. It is a story book with pictures, little one,' he said.

He opened the book and pointed to a picture and read the caption beneath it: 'Fuzzy Wuzzy Bear went for a holiday by the sea-side.'

The picture showed a gaily attired bear with the sea in the background. Suddenly the words 'sea' and 'holiday' leapt out at her and associated themselves with the picture. She did a little skip-dance around the old man.

'Read it again, Uncle,' she said, breathlessly.

She followed his finger intently as he read out the words. When he came to the word 'sea' she pointed to the sea in the picture. When he came to 'holiday', she pointed to the bright and carefree attire of the bear.

'What a clever child,' the old man said, laughing and excited too.

They read the whole book this way and she identified words he read out with the objects in the picture. Some of the objects, like roller-skates, were new to her and the old man had a hard time trying to explain what a roller-skate was. At last he said: 'Never mind, little one. I will try to find a roller-skate when next I go to town. It is better if you can see it and know how to use it.'

She took the book from him and went behind the tree to puzzle over it and absorb it. In less than a week she could read the simple captions beneath the pictures and understand the meaning of the words. The adventures of the bear became real too and she spent many hours sharing his experiences with him. When he ate an ice-cream, it was as though the melting cream dripped over her fingers. When he swam in the sea, she felt the wave rising to swamp her.

It was much harder to learn to read the letter book. It did not have pictures. Most of the words were meaningless strings of letters to her, and the old man, having a limited vocabulary, was unable to explain them.

One day the old man said gravely and sadly: 'Little one, I want you to keep the letter book. I am old and have no use for it any longer. It is now yours.'

She took the worn and soiled book that he offered her, and clasped it to her thin, flat chest. It made the old man laugh.

'In all my life I have never seen one as hungry for words as you.'

Two weeks later the old man died. The little girl was stricken and tearful for many weeks. She realized how little she could achieve on her own and how dependent she had been on the encouragement and guidance of the old man. She put the books aside and took long walks on her own, a silent, stubborn little figure possessed of an insatiable desire to learn to read and write, but not knowing at which point to start or where to go for knowledge. Strangely, it was her foster-father who thrust her out into a new way of life.

Each night she slept with Sarah and the man on a mattress on the floor. Sarah's husband was a taciturn man who seldom spoke. If he took a drink he always became violently ill.

One night the little girl awoke startled when a heavy hand was placed over her face almost smothering her. With the other hand the man tore at the thin and tattered clothing that she slept in. In her fright the child kicked out and struggled desperately and her struggles awakened the woman Sarah who shouted: 'My God, what are you doing to the child?'

He turned on his wife and beat her savagely. She did not cry out but long after he had returned to sleep, painful whimpers spilled out into the quiet of the room. The child crept under the wooden table and sat up the rest of the night trembling with the wild fright that possessed her.

The next morning Sarah's eyes and lips were puffed up and swollen but she did not refer to the incident of the night before.

At mid-morning she sent the child with a pail to fetch water at the tap a mile away from the slum. The child carefully set the pail down at the tap and continued walking. That night, bent almost double with weariness, she crept under a hedge and slept. Early the next morning she was up again, dizzy and faint with hunger and thirst but she feared to approach people in houses in case they questioned her. By midday she lost her sense of purpose and direction and only a silent, stubborn will-power kept her feet moving.

That night she reached a suburb of Cape Town and a man passing by noticed the weary, stumbling child and reached out a hand to detain her. A dazed, half-conscious face stared back at him for a moment. He caught her as she swayed and pitched forward in black unconsciousness. When she awoke the following morning, she found herself pinned down to a bed by the arms. A tube leading from a bottle on a stand beside the bed seemed to disappear somewhere inside her arm. She whimpered in fright.

'Now stop that,' said an efficient, exasperated voice close by her ear.

Soon it seemed as though these efficient, exasperated voices in rustling white starch were pounding and beating at her.

'Who are you?'

'Where do you come from?'

'Who are you?'

She gazed back at the exasperated faces with a dumb, animal fright.

'You should have seen the state she was in. We had to shave off her hair. It was matted with sores and riddled with lice.'

'Who are you?'

'What's your name?'

To all these questions she kept silent.

The hospital informed the police. Notices were placed in the paper but no one came forward to claim her. The case was handed on to a social worker; she was given a new name and birth date and registered as Charlotte Smith, born 6th January, 1939.

The social worker placed her with a family in the slums of Cape Town. The only difference between this slum and the one from which she had fled was that there was no refuse dump and reeking, stagnant water. The pattern of life was the same with the weekends of drunkenness and violence and the crude, animal, purposeless, crushing world of poverty. She learnt the lessons every unwanted stray has to learn:

Work hard. Do not answer back no matter what we do to you. Be satisfied with the scraps we give you, you cannot have what our children have. Remember we are unpredictable; when the mood gets us we can throw you out.

Until the age of sixteen she was placed and re-placed in ten homes.

During this time she had only three years of school. No one really bothered. It was generally thought that she was a dim-witted moron. Year by year she had become more and more silent and her inner retreat was almost to a point where no living being could reach her. The last home she lived in was the only one she remembered with warmth and affection. It was the home of a tailor and he sent her for the year that she lived with them to school with his six children. He was a member of the Communist Party and first thing every morning he made them sing 'The Internationale'.

The home was wonderfully peaceful and filled with a quality she had never experienced before: love and co-operation between a man and his wife. The wife was a quiet, unpretentious woman with eyes of a deep, clear, honey-gold brown. The man was intensely dedicated in everything he did and his belief in communism was childlike and absolute. From early morning until the late, lonely afternoon sunlight slanted into the room, he worked at his machine.

'You see,' he was fond of saying, 'the highest stage of living will be when every human being has enough to fulfil his needs.'

Communism itself had no meaning for her but when he encouraged her to read the protest literature he had accumulated, she read avidly because of the excitement words and books had always stimulated in her. One day, among all the pamphlets and protests, she found Darwin's theory of evolution and after that, in spite of the man's protests, read nothing else. The precise and logical arguments and the quiet, ecstatic beauty of the language never failed to awaken a delirious response in her. She absorbed it word by word for six months.

After a year the man's wife suddenly fell ill and died. She had to leave. The social worker told her that now that she was sixteen, the grant to support her stopped. She found work for her as a tea-girl in a hairdressing salon and a room in a large slum house occupied only by an old man and his wife. The arrangement made her feel peaceful and secure for the first time in her life. The old couple never bothered her and were in bed early each night. She paid very little for her room and whatever was left from her small weekly wage, she spent on books and writing materials. For the next four years of her life she sat up educating herself.

A trick of fate started her off in an eventful direction. One Friday evening as she returned home from work, she noticed a new paper on sale in the streets. Its bold type said: AFRICAN BEAT – *The Paper of the People.* Out of curiosity she bought it but later than night, as she read it, its emptiness and bold vulgarity shocked and surprised her. She had accustomed herself to the quiet and conservative tone of the daily newspapers. Impulsively she wrote a long letter of complaint and almost by return post received an astonishing reply. It said:

> *Dear Miss Smith,*
> *We thank you for your letter but regret that we are unable to publish it as the contents would be detrimental to the prestige of the paper.*
> *However, you strike us as a writer of no mean ability. We have recently opened a branch office in Cape Town and are desperately short-staffed. We would like to offer you a job. Should you find our offer agreeable, please call at our offices in Cape Town. We have already informed the Editor-in-Charge to expect you.*
> *Journalism offers endless opportunities for enthusiastic and enterprising young people.*

She stared at the letter almost in disbelief and had no doubt in her mind that she would apply for the job. The work she was doing was exhausting and unrewarding. The address they gave her was quite near to where she lived and early next Monday morning, instead of going to her work at the hairdressing salon, she went to the office of the newspaper, AFRICAN BEAT.

The office was on the fourth floor and as she stepped out of the lift she entered a half-open door. A long passage faced her. To her right were two closed doors. A light was burning overhead. At the far end of the passage a man paced up and down with the restlessness of a caged animal. She stood at the half-open door and looked at him uncertainly. He looked up, saw her and approached so swiftly and menacingly that a look of wild fear darted into her eyes. Unwillingly she stood her ground as he came up close and towered some two feet above her. He had a harsh, bony face with a sarcastic, down-turning mouth and a cruel glitter of amused contempt in his large, light brown eyes.

'What do you want, Mouse?' he asked softly but in the softness was a sting, cruel and barbed.

She handed him the letter and he read it and then looked at her a long while before he spoke again.

When he did his voice was gentle. 'This place is the last place "a writer of no mean ability" should come to.'

He swung around and opened a door nearest to them. 'PK, there's someone to see you.'

He handed her the letter as she passed him and closed the door behind her.

The man, PK, had brilliant blue eyes, a thick-set, hairy-looking body and a long ginger beard. When he spoke his voice had a slight squeak.

'Hello, Miss Smith. I've been expecting you. Please sit down.' He indicated a chair opposite him. 'Well, do you want the job?' he asked.

'Yes,' she said.

'Have you done any reporting before?'

'No.'

A look of comic despair came over his face. 'I can't handle the job of training a woman. I can't even manage them in my private life. Can you type?'

'No,' she said.

'Well you'd better spend the next few days teaching yourself. It's easy once you get the hang of the keys.'

The steady solemn gaze she directed at him began to make him feel uneasy.

'All right,' he said. 'I'll inform Head Office that you've accepted the job. Go into the next office and you'll find a spare desk and typewriter. That's for you.'

When she entered the office next door, the harsh-looking man was standing at the window. At a desk sat a short, muscular man with a dead-pan face and a permanent, cynical grin on his face. Both men battered her with the amused contemptuous looks in their eyes.

She looked back at them, impassive and aloof, unaware of the odd figure she cut in a dress too long and too big for her thin body.

The short man with the cynical grin said: 'Well, look what the cat brought in.'

The other man said: 'A Mouse.'

She walked quietly towards the spare desk.

'Hey, don't you introduce yourself?' said the cynical, muscular man.

'I've already introduced her,' the other man said. 'Her name is Mouse. Hello, Mouse. I'm Johnny. That dolt over there is James.'

The name stuck. From that day they called her Mouse.

2

There was a restlessness and intensity about Johnny that was hard to accommodate. None but the most indifferent or insensitive could tolerate being near him for long. He always seemed to be living at a perpetually intense level of concentration that was nerve-racking and destructive. He was a voluble talker too, and the slightest remark could set him off.

From a long habit of reserve and retreat she appeared to be indifferent to the battering effect of his personality, but this cold reserve seemed to drive him to extremes to taunt and provoke her. She fared no better with the other two men. James taunted her with sly, crude remarks and PK treated her with a patronising and paternal indulgence that was humiliating. To all their taunts she responded with a silent, impassive stare. Only to herself would she admit how they disturbed her.

Johnny had a spectacular way of entering the office each morning. He would turn the handle, thrust the door open violently with his foot and come in at a crashing pace. It had happened every morning for the six months she had been working there and each time it broke the continuity of whatever they were doing and placed James and her completely at his mercy.

Johnny could create a terrible tension in the room with his pacing. His restless, neon-like vitality seemed to say: 'Notice me! Notice me!' James usually gave in first and stopped whatever he was doing in a deliberate show of patient and patronising awareness. She tried for as long as she could but he would provoke her until she too had to admit an awareness.

This particular morning she kept her face rigidly stuck in the book she was reading but found herself consciously timing the pacing. It seemed to say: 'All right, Mouse. Pretend not to notice me. I can see

15

the effort is beginning to overwhelm you. Your hands are shaking. Why can't you be sensible like James and notice me?'

Pace. Pace. Pace.

'James, I dashed out another short story last night. Read it and tell me what you think about it. Catch!'

James caught it. 'Why don't you give up,' he said. 'You can't write. I don't even have to read this one to know it's about another prostitute walking down Hanover Street and shaking her behind. Where you see all these prostitutes is beyond me. I've never ever seen a prostitute walking down Hanover Street, shaking her behind. She wouldn't dare. The nearest I've come to it was a quite respectable, fat woman walking down the street in tight jeans – and everyone laughed at her. Can't you see that slum people are insanely respectable? No self-respecting prostitute would do what you say she does.'

'You think you can afford to criticise me? You think you're just great, huh? Pipe dreams! Junk! You're going nowhere. For about the past four years you've been trying to get the slum out of your system. When you eventually get it out you're going to adopt Mozart and Bach and Chopin as culture. And what then? You'll be a dead-end kid like you were six years ago. Your writing bores me to death. Every single story I've read of yours is about the happy little Coloured man and the colourful Malays. Why don't you leave that crap to those insane, patronising White women journalists who are forever at pains to tell the Coloureds how happy they are. Why don't you stay a dead-end kid and like it? It's a great life! It's much better than the sick stuff you're writing. And another thing. If you want culture, I might as well tell you that the musical form of Bach and Chopin is dead, dead, dead. It belonged to the age of drawing-room tea parties and fainting females. The music of today is jazz. Jazz is the only music that can reflect the speed and tempo of the age in which we live.'

'So what? You haven't convinced me of anything. All I heard was a big noise.'

'What the hell do I care about you, James. You're just a stupid clot with a thick hide.'

Johnny turned to his next target. 'Hello, Mouse. What are you reading today?'

He did not wait for a reply but grabbed the book impatiently and looked at the title.

'Electricity,' he said.

He kept quiet a while then said: 'Why do you read such complex things? The average reading interest of women your age is the fashion magazine and the true-love story.'

She looked back at him dumbly and impassively.

James said, 'Her reading habits are simple to analyse. She's afraid of everything. This great big dreadful world is too much for her. I suggest that the next book she buys be about sex so that she can overcome her fear of men. I was telling my wife only last night that I had an itch to go to bed with Mouse and she said I'd better do so and get it over with.'

Johnny laughed and watched her face close over and become dead in its expressionlessness.

The Editor, PK, walked in.

'When are you people going to get started on some work? I've been in my office for the past fifteen minutes and I haven't heard a stitch of work being done. Johnny, I want that story on the townships on my desk in fifteen minutes. You've been working on it long enough. Mouse, my dear. This copy is sentimental junk. When are you going to get it into your head that we are a filthy tabloid weekly. This paper is paying you only to write a dirty story. Remember that. I don't want to know that Mogamat Abdul was driven to peddle dope because he can't find work and has twelve children to support. That may make a good short story but it doesn't make our kind of news. Get some punch into it. Write it this way:

> *Mogamat Abdul is back in the jug again. He's been there sixteen times before – all because he cannot give up the dope racket. A Prison Department official said that the public should have no sympathy for Mogamat's type. They are hardened criminals and never seem to learn that crime does not pay. The gaol is there to protect law-abiding non-White citizens from such types.*

Get it?'

'Yes,' she said in her quiet, inarticulate voice.

'Then write it that way and let me have it in fifteen minutes. We have a deadline to meet. The only person who does any dog-work around here is James. Johnny, this paper does *not* pay you to stand and stare out of the window.'

'I'm thinking, PK,' and there was a sound of suppressed laughter in his voice.

'Go on. Say it. Let's hear it.'

'I'm thinking. White man throw Black man out of window. No news. Black man throw White man out of window. Plenty news.'

'Very funny. If you weren't such a good reporter I'd write to Head Office this very day and ask them to fire you. You're troublesome, destructive, quarrelsome and bad for the morale of the staff. Let me have that stuff in fifteen minutes.' He walked out slamming the door.

'Mouse,' Johnny said, gently, 'why don't you clear out of here and go and sit on the mountain and write your short stories?'

'Oh for Christ's sake, Johnny. Cut out the drama. Mouse is a sentimental slob and you know it,' James said.

'What's the use of getting mad with you, James. You are the typical fence-sitter who shuts both eyes to what is happening on both sides.'

The clatter of his typewriter exploded with sound.

TOWNSHIPS

How long is it all going to last? Recently, 80,000 people were moved out of the slums of the Cape into new homes. Another government township was established.

With the township the government built:

1 Butchery.

1 Dairy.

1 General Dealer.

1 Barber.

1 Beerhall.

The township is miles and miles away from any shopping-centre. In this ghetto 80,000 people have only:

1 Butcher where they may buy meat.

1 Dairy where they may buy milk.
1 General Dealer where they may shop.
1 Barber where they may cut their hair.
1 Beerhall where they may drink.
Dominating the scene is a large police station and barracks to
maintain the 'efficient management' of the township. The
township has a stark, naked look. The roads are dirt roads. The
houses are like those square boxes you see at a loading-zone,
empty of imagination or style. The only soft, light, colourful
touches in this atmosphere of doom are the pink, yellow and red
dahlias outside the police station.

When PK read it an expression of extreme annoyance crept over his face.

'Are you crazy? Head Office will never take this! I told you to get the human interest side: "Mrs Kumalo lived in a hovel all her life. She never knew what it was like to have a kitchen, privacy." etc.'

'Sorry, PK, I'm not a supporter of the government.'

'You don't have to talk that way. You know I'm on your side.'

'For Christ's sake, PK. We don't need your sympathy. You White leftists and sympathisers are the greatest supporters of the status quo. If you're so worried about freedom and justice for the underdog why don't you go and convert your White brothers and sisters who are causing all this mess and leave us alone.'

'Let's break it up, Johnny. I haven't got time for a political conference.'

'Sure. I just want to know if you're going to send up my story the way I wrote it.'

'You bet I will and I hope you get fired.'

'Sometimes I feel an affection for you, PK. You're a dirty White bastard and you don't mind showing it.'

PK just looked at him blackly. Johnny laughed and walked out, and started his restless pacing in the passage.

A few minutes later a door opened softly and Mouse appeared in the passage on her way to PK's office. He blocked her way forcing her to stop.

'Why are you going to hand in that crappy story to PK? Why don't you tell him to go to hell? Do you know what's wrong with this country? We've got twelve million meek, inarticulate, dumb people like you walking around. What do you think the Whites are doing. They're fixing the clamps in tighter. Anyone who has a mind to change the system will have to change you first. And another thing. Since you've been around you've upset the peace and order of this place. We were getting along fine without you. PK is my best buddy but I find myself fighting with him every day. Who's to blame? You. You've got a nervous disorder that's infectious. You pretend to walk around like an iceberg when all the time you're a powder-keg underneath. One day I'm going to reach the powder-keg and blow you to bits.'

He could gauge nothing from her expressionless face and sighed in exasperation. 'Do you know what you are? You're just a screwball, oddball crank that the loony-bin overlooked.'

Her mouth quivered slightly and she could not control the look of mute, intense hatred that darted out of her black eyes. He laughed, pleased that he had been able to provoke a reaction out of her and stepped aside to let her pass.

When she came out of PK's office Johnny was at the far end, lost in his private world, pacing and pacing. She walked silently and opened the door softly fearing that at any moment he would look up and shout at her.

PK opened his door and stuck his head out. 'I knew it,' he said. 'I just knew it. Why do you have to spend half the day pacing around in circles?'

'You shouldn't ask me questions, PK. I can be very frank.'

PK sighed: 'Go on, say it. Let's hear it.'

'I'm not just pacing. I'm thinking. I have to spend three-quarters of my life thinking for bastards like you who cannot think for themselves.'

A glint came into PK's eye. 'One of these days an unthinking bastard is going to put a bullet through you.'

'A lot have tried it already. I'm just a bit too quick for them.'

'There's always One Day. Come into my office. I have a job for you. I've just heard that ten people were burnt to death in a big fire that broke out in that slum area along the National Road. I've put Mouse on the job as I want her to get as much experience as possible. Go along with her and help her do the story and take the pics. Get all the gruesome details like burnt-out bodies, etc.'

'Why don'tyou put James on the job? I hate to be seen around with that woman. Her skirts are too long and the slip hangs out an inch all the way round.'

'Who's running the show here? You or me?'

'I'm not questioning your authority, PK I just said I hate to be seen around with that woman.'

'You don't have to walk next to her. You can tell her to walk on the other side of the road.'

There was a soft knock on the door and she entered with a cup of tea for PK. The two men stared at her in silence but she did not appear embarrassed. It was as though she was completely unaware of their amused scrutiny. When she closed the door, PK said, 'You're right. She's a sight.'

'She's a freak. There's something very wrong with her. I've a mind to put it right.'

Ten minutes later, as they went out into the street together, he said: 'You go and walk on that side of the road.' She turned and walked quietly across the road. He followed her and walked alongside.

'Why don't you tell me to go to hell?' he demanded. 'Ever since you've been around I've hardly heard six words come out of your mouth. What's wrong with you? Do you enjoy being shoved around?'

'I just don't care,' she said.

'That's a defeatist's attitude.'

She did not reply.

'Look,' he said. 'You can't go on living the way you do. Either somebody's going to mess you up or you'll do the job yourself. Your lack of fight is a challenge to a cruel and brutal world. You're available for anyone who wants a punching bag.'

She darted an angry look at him. 'Why don't you leave me alone?'

'I'm not interested in you as a person. I'm interested in what you

21

represent. Defeat. It provokes me. I'm the kind of man who can't kick a man when he's down. I want him to get up first.'

They caught the bus and did not speak further on the long journey out of town. The slum was much the same as the day on which she had left it. There was that familiar overpowering stench and the children scratching around on the refuse dump. The thin, hysterical dogs barked and the women crept out of the tin shacks to stare curiously. When they had collected all the details on the fire and he had taken the pictures, she paused a moment as they passed the shack where she had lived with the woman Sarah and her husband. A strange woman now stood in front of it.

'This is where I spent my childhood,' she said. 'I lived in this shack here.'

The information surprised him. 'Very few escape from conditions like this. How did you manage it?'

'Escape? I don't think I was trying to escape. I wanted to learn to read and write and it did not seem possible if I stayed here.'

He laughed.

'I think nothing can surprise me, and then life throws up something like you. You have a beautiful soul that was nurtured on a dung heap,' he said.

3

PK lived in a bachelor flat high up near the mountain. Johnny often visited PK. There was a streak of impetuousness and wild unreasonableness in PK that was very dear to his heart. Also, he could always be sure of PK's sympathy when an idea gripped him with feverish intensity. PK was not an anti-social man but he was inclined to get prickly and uncomfortable if anyone tried to get too close to him. Johnny's independence and self-centred egoism were therefore agreeable to him.

PK did not really care about the political situation one way or the other. He had a few comfortable habits and about the future he was like the lion who went to the same water-hole each day, never thinking that one day the water-hole might be empty of water. He was devoted to jazz, above all to the way it was played by Miles Davis. And, women liked him because his attitude to them was basically protective and gentle. He was a slight alcoholic too but could hold his drink well. Ever since they had been working together on the paper, a strong and comfortable friendship had developed between them. After work that day they sat in the flat together and drank in a companionable silence. PK was the first to break it.

'You know, Johnny? I'm getting tired of your unreasonableness.'

'But you can't change me, PK I was born that way.'

'In other words you mean that's an excuse for you to be as rude and aggressive as you like.'

'It's not. I only have one rule left as far as humanity is concerned. Either they take me as I am or they go to hell.'

'But you won't make out that way, Johnny. You have to take other people into consideration.'

'I could give you an analysis on just how much consideration some

23

people have for other people but, I don't feel quite up to it this evening. Life's rubbing me up the wrong way.'

'Do you know Mona?'

'Oh, for Christ's sake. Don't talk to me about women. I hate them. They mess everything up.'

'But Mona is a very interesting woman.'

'The trouble with you, PK, is that you're too susceptible. Can't you see how they're messing you up? You're looking quite dissipated. If you don't stop the pace you'll catch a disease.'

'You should talk. Your sex habits are disgusting.'

'Can't we talk about something else. Like jazz for instance.'

'I was thinking a while ago, Johnny, that half the trouble in the world is caused by the difficulty we have in communicating with each other. It's practically impossible to say what you really mean and to be sure that the other person is understanding you. Word communication is dependent on reason and logic but there are many things in life that are not reasonable or logical. A jazz musician can say something to me in his music but it would be quite beyond me to translate into words what he is communicating through music. What he has to say touches the most vital part of my life but I can only acknowledge his message silently.'

'I agree with you about the difficulty of coherent communication but we can't just let it go like that and throw up our hands in despair. Even if you say half of what you mean and someone half understands you, it helps a lot. It helps you to retain your sanity. We have a perfect example of insanity at the office in that dumb woman who never says a word. To all appearances she is completely dead. Even an illiterate, inarticulate person can find some way of communicating with others. She doesn't want to. Every time I see her, I just get a pain in the neck. If we were living in the Middle Ages I'd have agitated for her to be burnt as a witch and put an end to all the agony.'

PK laughed. 'The crazy system at Head Office has landed me with a big problem. Ever since she's been around I've been overworked. She's a talented writer but definitely not a news reporter. But definitely. Every single bit of copy she hands in sounds like a short story.'

'Why don't you tell her to clear out?'

'Be reasonable, Johnny. She has a living to earn, too.'

'But not in the lowest, cheapest, dirtiest form of journalism. Not even a genius could write the crap we have to write. Get her fired and you'll be saving yourself some overtime and doing her a great favour.'

'I admit she can't write the stuff we want but I'm not going to get her fired. I like the kid in a way. Ever since she's been around I've been fathering her. It makes me feel great: PK, sex-maniac, plays father to sweet young, innocent thing.'

'That's what baffles me. If you grew up the way she did you just would not stay sweet, young or innocent. She told me today that she started off life in that hell-hole off the National Road. It surprised me, because it's obvious she was not born there. The terrible thing about that slum is that it marks the people who have lived there, and bred and intermarried, with a facial structure and mentality that is like something inhuman. It's just an oozing, indiscriminate mixture of muck, incest and hell-fire. It stamps the individuals who live there so that they look like nothing on earth. That's why I say she was not born there and in some miraculous way escaped from that swamp. Everyone knows it's the dumping ground for illegitimate babies. I can only think that that applies in her case.'

'The government is trying to clear it up.'

'The new townships are just another hell from hell, PK. They're organized prison camps. On the average, incomes are so low that the people can hardly afford to pay these so-called sub-economic rentals. They live from day to day in fear of being dragged before the rent courts. Those who try to supplement their incomes by illicit liquor and other shady deals are constantly hounded out by the cops. A cop can enter a home any time the mood gets him. And what chances are there of raising the wages and standard of living when the economy of this country is based on cheap labour? It used to cost a man nothing to live in a shack in a slum. Now it costs him more than he can afford on his income to live in a township. The townships were built to remove the eye-sores, as the foreign tourists like to say. And incidentally to deprive those non-Whites, who were financially able, of their freehold rights and estates. The economists worked out that it would provide exploited – that's my word – people with a minimum standard of decent living but they never figured out what a human standard of living should be like.'

'What else can be done?'

'Who cares, PK? It's too much bother. They're a big black messy lot. Just herd them any way you like.'

'Now don't start that song again. We were having a pleasant time.'

'I sure hate to upset you with these unpleasant details.'

'You don't upset me, Johnny. There's a time and place for everything.'

'I only have time to think of how to blow this status quo to bits.'

'Let's get back to Mouse. Did she tell you any more about her mysterious past?'

'She didn't have to. It's written all over her face. Years of struggle, under-nourishment and a complete lack of love or happiness and that background has moulded her into something remote, unapproachable, inhuman and eccentric. And, do you know what? She's heading straight for disaster. Some human beings can get through life being remote, unapproachable, inhuman and eccentric because they're cold and heartless anyway. But she isn't. If she goes on like this much longer there's bound to be an explosion.'

'Why should you care?'

'Because she has guts and has achieved on her own what others can only achieve with the best education a university or college can give. It just happens that I feel strongly about this because I had to educate myself too, and I can't allow the enterprise she has shown to go to waste in a loony-bin.'

'Why don't you help her then?'

'You just ask simple questions, PK. How can you help someone you can't even reach mentally, emotionally or physically? I've pro-voked her, insulted her and she just retreats and retreats. I see it happening every time I talk to her. It drives me crazy.'

'Just say you could reach her, how do you plan to help her?'

'I'd just make love to her. Love is about the only thing that will make her normal again.'

PK laughed. 'You mean to tell me that you can't find a way to get her to bed?'

'I don't know where to start.'

'I never thought I'd live to see the day, Johnny.'

'It's difficult. You just tell me how.'

'It's not my problem, chum.'

'She has cut off all the normal approaches. Between her and the rest of the world is a gigantic wilderness full of little side paths that lead nowhere.'

PK shrugged helplessly. 'You baffle me. Here I thought you were a hardened cynic and all the time you're soft inside. It just doesn't add up. You just want to run around putting everything that *you* think is wrong right. The tap might be quite okay but you have to find a leak somewhere. Mouse strikes me as a normal human being, though a bit shy and reserved.'

'The trouble is, PK, you have only two pairs of eyes while I have four.'

'All I know is that you're dangerous. I just feel sorry for that poor kid. She doesn't know what's coming to her.'

4

The day was grey and bleak and rainy. She stood at the office window and felt crushed as she watched the relentless downpour of the late spring rain.

Click, bang, CRASH. And in burst Johnny like the sun. She turned.

'Hello Mouse,' he said breezily. 'I wrote another short story last night. Read it and then re-write it the way you think it should be. Make the people real. I want to give that bastard James a jolt out of his doltish complacency. I'm not a creative writer. I'm just doing this to keep that clot on his toes. He hates competition. He wants to be known as the only writer around here. You'd better show him you can do something, and better too. The kind of writing I'm concentrating on is going to get rid of governments and systems for good. There's nothing wrong with mankind. It's the systems mankind is forced to live under that cause all the mess. I'm going to fix these systems. Here. Catch!'

She caught it eagerly. His enthusiasm carried her along with it.

'There's no hurry, 'he said. 'You can do it in your spare time but try and let me have it by tomorrow morning if you can. Better put it away now. I think I hear James coming. I don't want him to catch on.'

Ten seconds later James walked in. 'Hello, you dumbheads,' he said pleasantly. 'For Christ's sake, morbid miserable Mouse is actually smiling. What gives?'

'She just told me that she's going to marry the king of Siam. They've been corresponding as pen pals for three years,' Johnny said.

'Oh hell.'

'The trouble with you, James, is that you lack originality. Your stupid doltish face reminds me of a mule. Why don't you give it all up and go graze in the field with the cows.'

'Funny thing. I was just thinking last night that you look like a wild mountain goat.'

'James, you owe me gratitude for stinging your sluggish mind into eloquence.'

PK stuck his ginger beard round the door. 'Morning slaves. Get cracking. We've got a deadline to meet. Come into my office, Mouse. I've got a terrific human-interest story for you to do.'

When she was seated opposite him, he cleared his throat and looked a bit uncomfortable.

'I want to know if you're happy doing the work you're doing now. It's no use sticking in a job if you don't like it.' She looked at him quietly and impassively.

'Don't you have anything to say?' he asked irritably.

'I am aware that I'm not doing very well.'

'Don't worry about that. You'll be okay once you get the hang of the work. Are you interested in politics?'

'No.'

'You're better off if you stay out of it. It's a dirty game. Well, that's enough of that. This Mrs Abrahams here wrote me a letter. She's a lonely old woman who has been bed-ridden for six years. She wants a wheel-chair and we've got to find her a wheel-chair. Ring up anywhere but get this wheel-chair. "*AFRICAN BEAT* – the paper with the big heart has done it again." See what I mean? Okay. As soon as you've found the wheel-chair let me know and we'll race around and get a pic of the old bird perched in it.'

PK made it sound such a simple matter. She rang up the Red Cross.

'Is she a deserving case?'

'I don't know.'

'We only give wheel-chairs to deserving cases and in any case we haven't any in stock.'

She rang up the Cripple Care.

'Is she a deserving case? We only supply wheel-chairs to deserving cases. Lots of these people apply to us for wheel-chairs when they can very well afford to buy their own. Sorry, we haven't any in stock.'

She rang St John's Ambulance.

'We'll put her on our list.'

'Could you please tell me if it would be possible to find one somewhere today?'

'Look lady. You're wasting my time. Wheel-chairs don't grow on trees.' Slam.

Johnny stopped the clatter of his typewriter. 'Mouse, why are you standing like that with the phone in your hand? Today is Wednesday, September 28th, 1959. It's ten o'clock. I'd like some coffee. Go and fetch me a carton from downstairs and get one for yourself.'

She walked out into the soaking rain, crossed the street and went into the café. It belonged to a cheerful, fat, lecherous man called Mohammed.

'Hello Chicken,' he said smiling as she entered. 'Would you like to see some French photos?'

'No.'

'Just look quick.'

In a distracted way she took the filthy picture-postcard he held out, and looked at it blindly.

'Nice hey?'

She handed it back to him.

'I'm looking for a wheel-chair.'

'You planning to go cripple, hey?'

'It's for the paper.'

'You people do crazy business there. No one want to buy AFRICAN BEAT from my shop anymore. They say it make out that the non-Whites bad.'

'Yes, I know.'

'Chicken, I don't know where you going to get a wheel-chair. 'He started to laugh, his fat stomach shaking up and down.

Her big black eyes stared at him across the counter with a look of profound melancholy and despair.

'You got a lot of troubles, Chicken, hee, hee.'

'Can I have two cartons of coffee. Leave one open. I'll drink it here.'

She turned and stared at the rain and had a panicky feeling about going to tell PK that she could not find the wheel-chair. Mohammed placed the coffee on the counter.

30

'Don't worry, Chicken. Maybe we will find the wheel-chair. I will ask the customers.'

She turned back to watch the rain. Its dismal, lonely bleakness seemed to comfort her. She was not aware that a customer had come into the shop until she heard Mohammed say, 'Excuse me, Sir, but would you know where's a wheel-chair? That young lady over there wants a wheel-chair.'

The customer looked startled and stared with suspicion at them.

'The lady work for a newspaper. She wants to do a story with a wheel-chair,' Mohammed explained smoothly.

'Why do you want a wheel-chair?' he asked in a hard, flat voice. His penetrating black eyes bored down into her and made her feel confused and uncomfortable.

'An old woman wrote to the paper and asked for a wheel-chair. The Editor asked me to find one,' she said, wondering if she should discuss this with a stranger.

The man thought it over a bit then said, 'Maybe I can help you. I have a grandmother who has a wheel-chair. She is too old to use it anymore. I could take you to her if you like. I have a car outside.'

'Thank you. I just want to deliver this coffee.'

He nodded curtly. Mohammed stood in the back-ground smiling respectfully. Well-dressed people always made him feel obliged to put on his most polite manner.

'Thank you, Mohammed. You're a great friend,' she said.

'Aw, you can tell me your troubles anytime, Chicken. I always got time for you.'

The man drove fast with an intense, silent concentration. The rain spattered on the windscreen and made her feel secure and comfortable in the fast-moving car. The house was quite far out of town and it took them about half-an-hour to get there. When the man's family heard what was wanted, they looked at each other in consternation. There was a feeling of sharp hostility in the air and she sensed it was directed at the man. After a bit of whispering together, a young woman spoke: 'It's true what my brother says. The old granny is not able to use it any longer but we do not like to give it away. We would not mind loaning it out for a few months. Before we can loan it out,

31

you must ask for permission from the old granny's doctor. I will give you his address but you must bring us a note from him authorising us to give it to you.'

She felt bewildered and humiliated by the woman's strange evasiveness. She looked at the man but his face was closed and impassive, waiting for her to decide.

'I'm sorry to have troubled you,' she said quietly.

'It was no trouble,' said the other woman smiling sweetly, but there was a sharp look of anger in her eyes.

When they were back in the car the man said: 'I'm sorry to have brought you right into the middle of a family quarrel but I was concerned about the wheel-chair. I thought they might overlook our differences, this time. I am the walking symbol of what they fear. Responsibility. Most people fear it. They look to the other man to do everything. I hoped you'd say what you did because if we had to call at the doctor's surgery, he would have said it was against his professional conscience. This other man, that everybody hopes will bear the responsibility for them, just isn't there most of the time; that is why the world progresses at such a slow rate. It is people like my family who prevent the world from progressing.'

He noticed out of the side of his eye that she was smiling.

'What amuses you?' he asked.

'The fact that you were driven to help me find a wheel-chair out of a sense of responsibility.'

'I have a fetish about it. The one thing in life that drives me around the bend is a display of evasiveness or irresponsibility, otherwise I like to pride myself on being a reasonable man. This fetish of mine also determines whom I accept as my friends so, as this world has a pitiful lack of responsible people, I also have a pitiful lack of friends. I just wish you were a man. You can accept responsibility. But since you are a woman I don't see how I can cultivate your friendship safely. Love is irresponsible and it's something that always seems to occur to some extent whenever a man and a woman associate. I would end up being torn between a responsibility for the love and the responsibility I feel towards my wife and children. My life is just one long dedication to responsibility. It can be rather lonely. I often try to laugh at myself but I'd be lost without responsibility. What fetishes do you have?'

'I don't think I have any,' she said laughing.

'That's because you are still quite young. Life determines your fetishes. It gives you knocks and drives you towards certain rigid forms of discipline. My craze about responsibility is a kind of discipline. Anyhow, what do we do about the wheel-chair now?'

'Thank you a lot for what you have done already, but I will just report that I can't find a wheel-chair right away.'

When she arrived at the office and told PK that she could not find a wheel-chair, he exploded: 'You've got to find that wheel-chair today! I've already informed Head Office that I'm sending up the story in the next news packet. Now, you do exactly as I say. Go and look for it in the slums around here. Knock on every door until you come to a house that has a wheel-chair. There are lots of cripples in the slums. Tell them we want to borrow it for one hour. As soon as you've found the damn thing let me know. It's two o'clock already. By the time we've finished with this mess it's going to be midnight. No one pays me for the overtime I do on stories you can't handle. Now clear out of here damn quick before I start busting everything up.'

◆

Although she was exhausted and tired, she sat up late that night working on the story Johnny had given her. The characters were sketchily and jerkily drawn and she used the brief ideas as clues to their form and individuality. Stiffly and uncertainly, like a child learning to walk, she wrote out her version of the story:

Sammy sat at the door of his home. The misery of degrading poverty was reflected in his eyes. There was no hope in them.

'I ain't even got a lousy penny for a fag,' he thought. A woman passed by. She looked like a cheap type of prostitute. When she noticed Sammy looking at her, she exaggerated the movements of her body. The woman reminded him of Nice Time, the taxi-driver and pimp.

'Ja,' thought Sammy. 'Nice Time got you all on his pay-roll. Going to get me a bus like Nice Time and pimp all the floozies.'

Suddenly Sammy's mother started screaming from inside the house. 'Sammy, you ol' good-for-nutting. When you going to get a job?'

Sammy hated his mother. Poverty does not allow for respect between mother and child. An unpleasant and unnatural intimacy is forced on them.

'Shut up, Ma,' Sammy said. 'I'm sick to death of your whining.'

He stood up and walked down the street to escape the sound of his mother's high-pitched, lisping, nagging voice. His walk was aimless and without direction and it irked him.

As he passed a dark alleyway, a voice called out to him. It was the old man, Five, leader of the most powerful gang in the district. Everyone called him Five because the five fingers of his left hand had been chopped off in a gang fight many years ago. Five had been pressing him to join the gang for some months now but he always refused. Sammy treasured his independence.

This morning, however, he was tempted. He had noticed that the boys in Five's gang were never without cigarettes or money. Five was well known for his generosity with money.

'How's things?' Sammy asked.

The old man looked at him shrewdly. 'What you aiming to do, Sammy? Start a club of your own?'

'Why you so worried about my plans, Five?'

'I got to give the orders around here. I got to be the boss. Everyone got to join my club.'

The boy looked at him insolently. 'Nobody shoves me around. I'm on my ace,' he said.

'We don't stand for it. You got to make up your mind. You got to join,' Five said.

'I make up my mind already. I'm on my ace,' Sammy said.

'They was telling me you spying for the law. What you got to say to that?'

'You know what I got to say. Shit!'

A peculiar smile flickered into the old man's eyes. 'There got to be one leader. I got to control everything and nobody got to give me back answers like that.'

'I just tell you I'm on my ace. I don't want to control nobody and nobody got to control me,' Sammy said.

He walked down the street whistling carelessly but the craving for a cigarette was very strong so he stopped by a Fish and Chips shop. It was owned by a Polish immigrant, Mr Pollak; a rough-talking, down-to-earth man with a generous heart and a happy, optimistic outlook on life.

'Can I help you out today, Mr Pollak?' Sammy asked.

'Sure Sammee,' he said in his cheerful, booming voice. They had been friends for many years and one strong point that Sammy found they had in common was women, but, Sammy doubted if Mr Pollak liked women for the same reasons that he did. Women had the effect of making Mr Pollak eloquent and poetic. He was a sucker too for pretty, feminine smiles and never seemed to notice how many packets of fish and chips he gave away each day. Sammy's appreciation of women was of a very different nature. Their bodies fascinated him. They were so different from his. The way they reacted to him too provoked, excited and intrigued him. He just had to look at them and they would stammer and blush. Sometimes if he got a girl alone at night on a dark street-corner he would trap her up against a wall just so that he could feel the soft and surprising curves of her body. It could make him fall into a dizzy ecstasy.

He busied himself energetically cleaning the fish in the back of the shop.

'One day,' he thought, 'I'm going to get me a ship.' Mr Pollak disturbed his daydream.

'Sammee. Come see. This ladee breeng me a *kat*.'

The pretty creature, a little black kitten, sprang out of Mr Pollak's arms and sat on the counter looking at its new home with an air of ownership. The gesture delighted Mr Pollak and he stroked the cat lovingly.

Sammy stared at the girl. She dropped her head shyly, then looked at him from under her eyes. She was pretty too.

'What are you doing tonight?' Sammy asked her.

'Nothing,' she said.

'How about you and me going somewhere?'

'My Ma don't let me go out with boys,' she said.

'My Ma don't let me go out with girls,' he said teasingly. She giggled nervously.

'Maybe I'll see you around here, seven o'clock,' he said.

'Maybe,' she said.

He watched her legs as she walked out of the shop. They were smooth, brown, long and slender and tapered elegantly towards the ankles. Again Mr Pollak disturbed his dreams.

'What name we give for the *kat*, Sammee?'

'Seven o'clock, Mr Pollak,' he said smiling.

'Savan o'clock? Ha, ha, ha. How do you do, Savan o'clock. Do you vant som feesh?'

The cat bent over and licked its back vigorously in assent.

'Never was a *kat* like this,' said Mr Pollak, laughing tenderly. 'Breeng som feesh for Savan o'clock, Sammee.'

The girl was at the fish shop at seven o'clock that night. She had on a bright yellow print skirt and scarf.

'Hallo, sweetee,' said Mr Pollak lovingly. 'You right on time, hey? What I wish for to be young again. Sammee! The ladee is here.'

Mr Pollak gave Sammy a packet of fish and chips and a ten shilling note.

'Have good time, Sammee,' he said fondly.

Sammy took the girl to the cinema but they sat on the last two seats right at the back and hardly looked at the screen. She let him kiss her and feel her and after a time she started to feel him too. It shocked him.

'Don't do that,' he said sharply. She paid no attention to the command and once he had become accustomed to the idea, he found he liked the way she touched him. He had never yet found a woman as bold and daring as she was and when he took her home he insisted on seeing her again.

'Maybe,' she said.

For the first time he noticed the way the stars shone down between the narrow streets and the closely crowded houses. A few doors away from his home a number of figures detached themselves from the shadows. They were too many for him to fight and he let them pin him down by the arms and legs. One of them stood over him with a knife.

'Five say we must tell you you got to join,' the knife-holder said.

'Five knows what I got to say to that.'

'Five say we got to give you five minutes to make up your mind.'

'No need to wait five minutes.'

The knife shot down into the side of his neck tearing open a vein. The figures disappeared into the dark night. He could feel the hot blood forming into a pool about his head. He lifted his hand and pressed it into the wound but it continued to trickle through his fingers in hot sticky rivulets . . .

◆

The next morning she watched him with an almost childish eagerness as he read it through.

'Is this the first time you've written a short story?' he asked.

'Yes,' she said.

'I think it's damn good. For me at least you've made it come alive. Omit one or two details and it's a pretty accurate picture of what I was like about twenty years ago. I just gave you the scrappiest ideas to work on and you figured everything out in a way that I never would be able to. Writing reveals quite a lot about the writer. This bit here proves to me that you are very much alive inside. What makes you conceal this aliveness behind a mask of death?'

She did not reply.

'Do you think life will care about you if you do not show that you care about it?'

That impassive, blank look that he hated crept over her face. He felt a sharp upsurge of white-hot rage. 'I wish I could kill you,' he said fiercely. 'What's wrong with you?'

Her faint and whispered words were like a plea for mercy. 'Johnny, I just want to be left alone.'

'You dumb clot,' he said violently. 'Are you a part of life or not?

The more you try to retreat, the more life is going to bash at you. Why don't you get out of your shell and live! Why don't you start living, you dolt!'

James walked in.

'Hello,' he said pleasantly. 'Mouse getting it in the neck again? What's she done this time?'

Johnny turned an him fiercely. 'Here. Catch! I wrote another short story last night. Read it!'

'Oh Lord. I told you I didn't want to read the crap you write anymore.'

'Read it!'

'For Christ's sake, Johnny. If you've got a gripe against the world don't try to take it out on me.'

PK stuck his ginger beard around the door. He looked in a black mood. 'When are you bastards going to get cracking. We've got a deadline to meet. Come into my office at once, Mouse.' He slammed the door. She walked to it and closed it quietly after her.

'You see?' James said, 'Mouse has done it again.'

'Why do you ever bother to open your mouth? Each time you do I become convinced that you are feeble-minded.'

James grinned. 'You know where you can go,' he said.

'You just shut your mouth and read that story. Mouse wrote it. I think it's damn good and you'd better say so too.'

'Has it ever occurred to you that you're overbearing and detestable?'

'I have to be with clots like you.'

In his office PK burst out: 'Look here, Mouse. I've had it with you! I've just had it! You bungle every job I put you on. Do you think I enjoyed pulling that trick on the old bird? You see that you ring up these charities every day until one of them gives her a wheel-chair. Your lack of initiative and enterprise is driving me crazy. Do you think journalism is a party game? No journalist in his right mind comes back to the office and admits that he can't do a story. I have half a mind to get you fired but I'm giving you one last chance. I'm putting you on courts. All you have to do is sit in that court room and take down the details. Ready-made stories. You won't have to go out and look for them and I won't have to do anymore overtime. From the Magistrate's Court I want immorality cases and from the Supreme Court I want death sentences, and I want at least one story brought in every day. Now get out of here before I start throwing something at you.'

As she passed on her way out, Johnny was in the passage doing his usual amount of daily pacing. 'What happened?' he asked. 'Why is PK mad with you?'

She just looked at him in a blind way and walked on.

'What the hell do I care,' he thought.

PK stuck his beard out of the door. 'Why aren't you doing any work?'

'For Christ's sake PK, I have to think the thing out first. The issue is complicated.'

'You and your bloody thoughts. We've got a deadline to meet. When no work comes in, Head Office puts the pressure on me.'

'Okay, you don't have to be mad with me too.'

'Who told you I'm mad about anything? I just want some work done around here. Get cracking.'

When Johnny went back to his desk he noticed that James had placed the short story on his typewriter.

'What do you think of it, James?'

'It's nothing very brilliant,' James said seriously. 'But it has some vivid moments. The ending is weak. It just fades out. I suspect that it must have involved a bit of feeling to write that. I never expected Mouse to be capable of feeling. She looks pretty dead.'

'You look pretty dead too. Why talk junk to me. Can't you say the thing is either good or bad? I think it's damn good.'

'I haven't your enthusiasm or emotionalism.'

'You care about this writing game, James?'

'Yes.'

'Then let me give you some advice.'

'I don't need any, thanks.'

'I'm giving it to you all the same. Don't be a martyr. You're killing yourself and your writing by trying to get the slum out of your system.

What does it matter how a man grew up? What matters is Now, the present. It's futile to grind an axe about the past.'

'I don't think we can throw off the past entirely, Johnny. Although you do not credit me with more intelligence than a mule, I'm pretty good at character reading and I'm almost hundred per cent sure that something that happened to you in the past is still eating you up. You come from the same environment that I do and there are things that happened that marked me for life. I just cannot obliterate the scars. In my case it was the violence. I hate violence. It is blind and savage. Violence is a small matter to you. You are by nature violent and can return blow for blow, so that wasn't your problem. Would you like me to take a guess at what's eating you up?'

'Sure.'

'Christ, Johnny. It sticks out a mile. It was a woman.'

'How did you figure that out?'

'Simple. You have the kind of masculinity that women find irresistible. Being emotional you take love seriously so . . . a woman gave you a knock when you were too young to protect yourself; so, forever after you have to take out your gripe on womankind. I happen to move around in the salacious underworld of sex and I've heard some great stories about you. The fact that you've been messing up high-society bitches proves that it was one of them who gave you the knock. Do I have to explain further?'

'No.'

'Thanks. I like to reserve my probing for my novels. One day I will have to write a book about you.'

'Save yourself the trouble. My life isn't a best-seller.'

'You interest me. I've almost got you all figured out. There are just one or two pieces that don't fit.'

'Like what?'

'Your desire for a cause and the game you're trying to play with Mouse.'

'Glad to know I've still got something left that you can't figure out.'

'Why don't you leave the kid alone? She's half crazy already. It just needs someone like you to mess her up and she'll go round the bend completely. If you're just looking for fun, there are plenty of tough women who can take your kind of fun.'

'I've heard enough of your smart talk. I'm not listening anymore.'

'Credit me at least with acute observation, Johnny.'

'You're the most despicable type of fence-sitter. A parasite. You may have acute observation but you use it for your own sly and secretive aims. You say I should leave Mouse alone? I'm telling you that you had better if you want to stay in one piece.'

James grinned cynically and inscrutably and turned back to his typewriter. Johnny stared down at the short story. It and the conversation evoked uneasy, haunting memories . . .

5

Young and extremely poor, he might have been attracted to Five's gang as so many other young men in the neighbourhood had been drawn into it for those reasons. It was a way of earning quick money with a little risk and adventure attached to it. But, he resented any form of control and was rebellious against carrying out the orders of another. Five attained his sense of power and dominance through the numerous subjects who unquestioningly carried out his orders. It got so that any form of independence was a threat to Five's power and prestige; he could not allow Johnny to stand free from his control. His resistance to such a powerful man could only end in his death, so when Five started pressing him to join the gang he quietly left the district one night and joined a small group of fishermen who lived a wild, tough and hazardous life sleeping in rough shacks on the beach and watching the sea, watching the tides and watching the weather; silent, taciturn, hermit men. The only contact they ever had with the town was in the brief trips they made each day to sell their fish at the fish-market. Early each morning, weather permitting, they would pull out with the tide in small boats and cast their nets in deep sea. Then they would return to the beach with the late afternoon tide. At night they drank hard and silently and fell into an exhausted sleep.

The life was like a slow death to him. It completely absorbed his restless, youthful vitality and the long silent hours spent on the vast, monotonous roll of the sea dazed his mind. It was as though the exhausting demands of the work were slowly changing him into something rigid and elemental like a dry, bleak tree that has been battered to death by exposure to fierce winds and storms; yet it was his only, and temporary, refuge from a sudden and violent death and hopeless, abysmal, crushing poverty.

The night alone, and the slow passage of the stars, could bring him briefly to life again. He often slept out on the beach, lying on his back and watching the stars, soothed by his utter and complete isolation and even immune to the ceaseless pounding of the sea below him. He loved the dawn too, for then the sea would be quiet and flat and still, and there would be clear green pools between the exposed, black, jagged sea rocks. He always arose early so that he could bathe in the clear, cold water.

One early dawn a young woman came walking along the beach. She was barefoot and her long black hair hung loosely behind her. She was tall and very thin and walked in a direct and purposeful way with long, swift strides. She was suddenly halted in her walk as he rose out of a pool and picked his way carefully between the sharp, cutting, slippery rocks. The long sinewy muscles of his legs moved with a taut control and the smoother muscles of his hard sea-burnt, sun-burnt body seemed alive with a vital and youthful power.

'How beautiful,' she whispered and looked at him the way anyone would look when momentarily carried away and uplifted by the sight of a beautiful object.

He looked up as he reached the sand and saw her. A year of sea-daze and hard labour had numbed his senses and he was hardly conscious of his nakedness. His look was one of blank amazement. She looked like an unearthly apparition in the early morning light and her small, thin face with abnormally large black eyes was as sombre as a grey storm sky. Her wild black hair clung around her shoulders and down her back.

He bent and pulled on his rough worn pants and a faded navy-blue jersey, then, without another look in her direction turned and walked to where the fishermen were grouped around a small fire, waiting for the coffee-water to boil. She followed him and when he looked up again she was sitting a little distance away gazing out to sea.

The fishermen noticed her too but she did not disturb them. They had long lost the capacity to respond to anything but the fish and the unpredictable moods of the sea. She felt his gaze on her and turned her head and looked at him directly with large demanding eyes. It intrigued him. He picked up a mug of coffee and walked over to her. She accepted it with a quick, darting glance of her large, dark eyes.

43

'Thank you,' she said in a firm, low-toned voice.

He sat down a little distance from her. He was still surprised at her unexpected appearance. Also, she frightened him a little. It may have been her long, wild hair or the strangeness of her eyes that were bold in a way that was different from the way any other woman had looked at him.

'What is your name?' she asked, just for something to say.

'Johnny,' he said.

'I'm Ruby,' she said, then added, 'my father gave me that name. He says I am the flame of his heart. We are extremely fond of each other.'

As he said nothing to that she talked on, half to herself, in her beautiful, low-toned, murmuring voice.

'You men are so silent,' she said. 'You walk as though you are blind and deaf and dumb. Somehow it blends well with the silent majesty of this morning.'

He looked at her in surprise. 'It is the sea that kills us.'

'You mean,' she said, 'it's killing you. Those men love the sea. They are here because they want to be. You are here for other reasons. You have run away from something and are hiding here.'

'I don't like the way you talk,' he said sharply.

'Why?'

He saw the men moving to prepare the boats. 'I want the cup,' he said.

'But I haven't finished.'

'Hurry up,' he commanded.

'I can't drink as fast as you. I'll burn my mouth.'

He looked at her contemptuously. 'You talk too much, that's why,' he said.

She bent her head to hide a smile and poured the coffee out onto the sand. He half-snatched the cup out of her hand. He did not look at her all the time they busied themselves with the boats, carefully manoeuvring them between the exposed rocks with oars. When they reached deep sea he looked up and she was standing on the beach looking toward them. The swell of the sea suddenly hid her from sight.

She came every morning after that but he ignored her, never once

44

looking her way. One of the men would always take her a cup of coffee. The silent, taciturn fishermen would even turn and nod politely as she came up and sat a little distance away from them. Only when out at sea would he look up and she would always be standing there, looking, waiting. Once she raised her hand slightly.

He awoke one morning to find her standing and looking down at him in her silent, sombre way. It was still quite dark with only the faintest hint of dawn in the sky. He lay on his back looking back at her, unmoving. She dropped down on her knees beside him.

'Why do you ignore me,' she whispered.

'Go away,' he said, without turning his head. She placed a trembling hand on his chest and he turned his head and saw that she was crying silently. He pulled her to him and her wild hair fell across his face and neck.

'Love me! Love me! Love me!' she cried and it seemed as though his love was as fierce as the savage, battering beat of a high sea; or, like a storm beating down on the dry, hard earth of her body and she absorbed its pounding drive, lost and lost in an elemental ecstasy; and then, like the sweet shuddering sigh of the satiated earth, their limbs enclosed about each other in a close and relaxed embrace. She moved her hand caressingly down his back.

'It's so strong and deeply curved,' she said.

He looked at the two dark wings of her eyebrows and the smooth stillness of her dark brown face. 'Where did you grow up?' he asked.

'On a farm,' she said. 'We had a rose garden and I used to walk through the garden swinging a stick at the ground. At the bottom of the garden were little people about three inches high and they used to talk to me.'

Nothing that she said surprised him. She was altogether too strange.

'Where did you grow up?' she asked.

'In a town,' he said.

He sat up. 'The boats will be leaving soon,' he said. 'It's my turn to light the fire for the coffee.'

She sat up beside him. 'Johnny,' she said earnestly, 'I love you.'

He turned his head away with a shy gesture. She looked at him wonderingly and said softly: 'I've never seen a man do that before.

The men I know are too superficial to be capable of something like that.'

They walked together to the fishermen's shacks and she helped him to light the fire; then, as the fishermen awoke and came to sit around it, she moved a distance away. They greeted her silently like an old and familiar friend and she acknowledged their friendship with a solemn and queenly dignity. When the coffee was ready he walked over to her with two cups and sat down.

'Do you have another woman?' she asked.

'No,' he said and a gleam of laughter shone in his eyes.

'I was worried,' she said. 'You have a magnetic physical attraction.'

'Why do you talk so much?' he demanded.

She bent her head smiling. 'You are very rough with me,' she said. 'Not even my father talks to me the way you do, but I like it. Often those who talk softly and sweetly hide a stabbing cruelty in that softness and sweetness.'

She looked at him in a sudden fierce and intense way. 'Oh Johnny! I love everything about you. The way you hold up your head so high and independently and the way you walk, as though you were a king. Please kiss me. The fishermen won't notice.'

That night her face seemed to blink down at him from the stars and he could not sleep. He stood up and walked along the sea's edge.

'Ruby,' he said, restlessly. 'Ruby.' And she came, running along the beach towards him and clung to him tightly, her thin body vibrating with passion.

'Did you call me?' she asked.

'Yes,' he said.

'I was in bed already but I heard you so clearly that I got up and came immediately.'

They pursued their love with a wild abandon, unprotected against the treachery of the insecure foundation on which it was based and too young to bridge the gap that would suddenly and unexpectedly fling them miles apart. For him it was like a high and glorious summer in the bleak winter of his life and for years afterwards the memory of her strange beauty and the hard, vibrating passion of her body lived with him like an unhappiness that could not die. For her it was the tragic responsibility of having destroyed the one thing she had sought from life with a desperate and violent intensity. Devastated and broken, she lay for days half-conscious while her family wondered in shocked silence at her sudden collapse.

Eventually her mother called a doctor as she could not make her answer questions. The doctor misunderstood the cause of distress but what he told her rallied her fast-ebbing strength for a while.

'You must pull yourself together,' he said. 'Lots of young girls get babies before they are married.'

'I am to have a baby?' she asked, a flicker of interest creeping into her eyes.

The doctor was surprised. 'You mean to tell me you don't know? You're about four months pregnant already.'

'I never thought about it,' she said.

'What's the cause of your collapse, then?'

She did not reply. He smiled and patted her hand gently. 'I think I can guess,' he said. 'Something went wrong with the love affair.'

Her sudden tears told him that his guess was correct.

'That happens to lots of other young girls too. Love is always difficult for the very young. It is hard at your age to foresee the consequences and it is the one thing that always brings consequences. We have to think of the child now. Would you like me to inform your mother or would you like to tell her yourself?'

'I think you had better tell her. She will not understand.'

'She will. She was young once, like you. You need help. You are endangering the life of the child.'

He was mistaken about that too. Her mother came in soon after he had left and spoke to her with a cold fury. 'How did you get this way? Haven't I warned you? Haven't I told you everything about life?'

She looked back at her mother without interest.

'Who is the man?' her mother asked.

'Someone you will never know,' she said quietly.

'I could have known you would do something like this,' her mother said, bitterly. 'You've given me nothing but trouble with your stubborn, headstrong ways. I cannot allow you to bring disgrace on your sisters and the home. He will have to marry you. I'll make him marry you.'

'How?' she asked.

'You just give me his name and address.'

'I will not,' she said.

'Oh God. Why did this have to happen to me? I cannot even appeal to your father. He walks around with his head in the clouds. Be sensible, Ruby. It's a disgrace to have a child when you're not married. I will never to able to hold up my head again if this gets known.'

'Please leave me alone. I'm suffering enough.' She turned and hid her face in the pillow, crying quietly.

It was only to her father that she could talk of the agony that was torturing her. He was a quiet, aloof man, absent-minded and detached from reality; shy and awkward and undemonstrative; a constant source of irritation to his wife and a stranger to most of his friends and children. In the evenings he could always be found in a quiet corner of the house painting delicately beautiful water-colours of landscapes or flowers. In a passionless way he acknowledged a kinship with his daughter Ruby and she was the only one of his seven children who had been able to penetrate the wall of indifference and detachment that permanently surrounded him.

That evening he came and sat quietly at her bedside. The unruffled calm of his personality soothed and comforted her.

'Dad, do you know that I'm going to have a baby?' she asked quietly.

'Yes,' he said. 'Your mother told me.'

'Is it a disgrace?' she asked.

'No. Women were meant to have babies,' he said with his quiet, gentle smile.

'But I'm not married?'

'It's all right,' he said.

'Oh Dad. Nothing is ever wrong to you. I've really done something wrong. I don't mean about getting the baby. It's something more terrible than that and for the past two weeks I've felt as though I was dying.'

'You take things too much to heart.'

'But you just don't know. You just haven't the faults that I have. The greatest crime in this world is to be a moral coward. I am a moral coward. I rejected a man I love simply because in the eyes of others he would appear poor and lowly. He is poor. He is just a homeless fisherman who sleeps on the beach but inwardly he is the kind of man who walks as though he is a lord of the earth. I could acknowledge him for what he was but I found that I could not make this acknowledgement at all times, especially when an occasion arose when it was most necessary to do so. Do you know Paddy, Dad?'

'No.'

'He comes here often. He is my dancing partner. Paddy proved to me that I was not really worthy of the love of this man. About two weeks ago I was standing on a street corner talking to Paddy and saw him walking towards us with a large bunch of fish in his hand. The only thing I could think of was how ashamed I would be for Paddy to know that I had associated in any way with a man who was of such a low social standing. I just pretended I had never met him, but I could not pretend to him. I knew he knew that I was ashamed of him because he was not dressed in a suit like Paddy and carried fish in his hand. I couldn't help seeing the look of contempt in his eyes as he passed close by. It showed me how hollow and superficial I really am.'

'It's not too late to put matters right. Go to him and say you are sorry. He loves you too and will forgive you.'

'Oh Dad. I cannot. I dare not. He is too proud and independent. We had a way of communicating with each other but it's all cut off now. He does not call to me anymore.'

'My dear one. I wish I could help you,' her father said helplessly.

In the tortuous months that followed, her mother kept her a prisoner in her room, anxious to conceal her state of pregnancy from friends and neighbours.

'Never leave the house,' her mother said. 'I have told everyone that you are away on holiday. You've brought this trouble on yourself so you must pay for it now.'

The days passed in a listless daze. She lost interest in the child and became deaf and blind to everything but the crying ache somewhere inside her. There was no way to assuage or remove it. With each new day it began its clamour.

When it was almost time for the baby to be born, her mother said, 'When the child is born you will have to give it away. Your friend, Paddy, wants to marry you but he does not want the child. He is willing to take you to another town where you can forget what has happened. You will never get another chance like this. Men do not like to marry women who get babies out of wedlock. Paddy is making you a decent offer under the circumstances. Do you accept?'

'Yes,' she said.

'I have made arrangements for the child. Sarah, the woman who does our washing, will take it. She has no children of her own. I have already bought the clothes for the baby and given them to her. The doctor told me that it will be any day now.'

'I would like to speak to Paddy,' she said.

'What about?' her mother asked suspiciously.

'I just want to talk to someone. I've been sitting here for months without anyone to talk to.'

'It's your own fault. It's not as though you did not know what you were doing. You had better not say anything to Paddy that will make him change his mind.'

'I will not,' she said.

'All right. I'll send word for Paddy to come around.'

They had been dancing partners and casual friends for many years. Paddy was a tall, bony young man with restless black eyes and a less than average intelligence but, unlike her mother who was in the habit of overriding other people's feelings, the moment he entered the room he noticed the bright feverish look in her eyes and the dark smudges of sleepless nights beneath them. It made him tug at his tie awkwardly.

'Hello Ruby,' he said with an uncomfortable smile.

'Hi Paddy,' she said quietly.

'That doesn't sound like the girl I used to know. Snap out of it, Honey. Everything's going to be okay.'

She moved her lips in a painful grimace, and he averted his eyes from her large abdomen.

'Who's the swine who did this to you?' he asked.

'What do you mean?'

'I mean a man can have his fun but the woman has to bear everything.'

'I see. Well he is not a swine, Paddy. He is a fisherman and I love him.'

He laughed uncertainly not knowing how to take her statement.

'My mother told me you wanted to marry me. Is that true?'

'Yes,' he said.

'Why?'

'I've always wanted to marry you, Ruby.'

'Why?'

'You're the kind of woman who won't drag a man down.'

'What do you mean?'

'I mean some women drag a man down because they don't know how to value his good name. You're not that kind of woman. With you I can get somewhere in the world.'

'I see. Maybe that's all I deserve, Paddy.'

'Cheer up, Honey. It won't be so bad once it's all over. We'll go away to another town as soon as you are able to travel.'

The baby was born three days later. It was a girl. For a few happy days the child distracted her from the clamour of that unceasing ache which had become an intolerable burden to her. It seemed as though she could never have enough of gazing at the minute perfection of her tiny, pink finger nails and toes and mouth. Once, as she held the baby cradled in her arms, its great black eyes opened briefly and appeared to look at her possessively. She felt a wrenching agony.

'Why do I have to lose you too?' she cried, but her cry was lost in the empty, darkened room.

Paddy drove her to the slum along the National Road. On the way he told her that he wished them to leave that night and once they had reached the town where they were to live they would be married quietly and privately. She agreed to everything but the life within her was already cold and dead. Her outward calm deceived him, also the unfaltering way in which she walked toward the shack houses to hand over the baby to the woman, Sarah.

When they reached home she said she wanted to leave immediately.

'Let me help you with your packing, dear,' her mother said, smiling in relief now that the cause of her anxiety was to be removed.

'No thank you, Mother. I can manage. I won't be long, Paddy. Maybe half-an-hour.'

Neither her mother nor Paddy took particular notice as she walked to the kitchen and selected a small knife with a sharp, thin blade. Concealing it in the palm of her hand, she walked with her long, swift stride to her room and locked the door. With quick, deliberate movements she slashed deep into her wrists . . .

6

It was Friday morning and the weekend edition of AFRICAN BEAT had just reached the office. Johnny paced up and down with his copy. In a prominent place on the front page was a picture of a smiling old woman in a wheel-chair. A bold caption read: AFRICAN BEAT – THE PAPER WITH THE BIG HEART – HAS DONE IT AGAIN.

'Did you do this story, Mouse?' he asked abruptly.

'Yes,' she said.

'Did the woman really get the wheel-chair?'

'No.'

'I knew it. I knew something dirty was going on. You and your despicable weakness! How could you let PK shove you into something like this? He is just an unscrupulous White bastard. All he thinks about is the story and he does not mind what he does to get it.'

James turned around.

'Why don't you blame Mouse for a change? You're always defending her. She must have been messing around on the day she was supposed to be doing the story. I saw her getting out of a car and the man inside held her hand for about three minutes.'

'Is this true, Mouse?'

'Yes.'

'So that's what you do! During working hours you run around with men in cars.'

'But I wasn't running around. I just met the man for the first time in Mohammed's cafe. Mohammed told him I was looking for a wheel-chair. He told me he had a grandmother who was too old to use her wheel-chair and offered to take me there to get it but the family did not want to give it away.'

'Why did he have to hold your hand?'

'I don't know.'

'He must have had a reason and you'd better explain.'

'I tell you, I don't know why. He was talking to me about responsibility all the time and the reason why he helped me to find a wheel-chair was because he liked accepting responsibility.'

'Mouse, you are a clot. Did he say he wanted to see you again?'

'No.'

'Now where's the mystery, James? If you're not careful that loose mouth of yours will get you into serious trouble. The blame for this muck goes to PK. Mouse did her best to get a wheel-chair, even to the extent of jumping into the car of a strange man and risking her life for a rag like this. What would have happened if he was a sex-maniac or something?'

'Sir Galahad, you're making me sick.'

'Of course. The only interest you have in a woman is in someplace unmentionable. I wonder how good you are at the performance. Men with loose sex habits are usually bad performers.'

'I've heard a story or two about you.'

'Thanks, I know how good I am.'

PK stuck his beard around the door. 'Morning slaves,' he said cheerfully.

'PK, where's your conscience?'

'What do you mean?'

'Why don't you come into the room. A man who peers around doors has got psycho trouble.'

'Look Johnny. If you want to pick a fight, don't start with me. I can be unreasonable first thing in the morning.' He walked into the room.

'I'm not picking a fight. I just want to know why it is stated here that the paper gave this woman a wheel-chair when in reality it did not.'

'Ask Mouse.'

'I've already asked her. Now I'm asking you.'

'Oh for Christ's sake. I put Mouse on the job and she runs around the whole day and tells me at two o'clock that she can't flnd a wheel-chair. I'd already informed Head Office that I was sending the story in the next news packet.'

'How typical, PK. How typical of secluded White mentality. You are so accustomed to getting the best in the land that you think you can just sit around and give orders. Wheel-chairs are hard to come by. When you say Mouse was running around you just don't know how hard she tried to find the damn thing, even to the extent of jumping into the car of a strange man because he said his grandmother had one. Some terrible things have happened to women who have jumped into strange cars. But could you care? Oh no. Like I always tell you, you're a dirty White bastard, PK.'

'Look here. I won't have you calling me names!'

'Why not, when it's the truth?'

'What does one do with a person like you? You're troublesome, quarrelsome and bad for the morale of the staff. If . . .'

'. . . you weren't such a good reporter I'd write to Head Office to fire you. Please get me fired, PK, I've had it with this crappy joint.'

'Why don't you fire Mouse instead, PK? She's the one who's caused all this mess.'

'Look here, James. I'll ask for your advice when I need it. I'm still in charge around here, even though it looks very doubtful.'

'I'd like to bash that doltish, mulish face of yours, James. PK is responsible for this mess and you know it. And PK knows it too, only he hasn't got the guts to admit it.

'I wonder why a drip like you has suddenly become the ardent defender of females.'

'James, this is no place to make personal remarks. You can make them in a pub or a toilet but this is a newspaper office and the sooner you realize that, the better it will be for you. I don't like that remark you made just now, Johnny. I can admit it was a lousy thing to do to the old bird. I even told Mouse so. She is ringing up these charities every day until that woman gets her wheel-chair. And another thing. I didn't mean one damn about getting you fired. Frankly, I'd be lost without you. I take it everything's settled now. I've had enough of showdowns for one morning. It's time some work was done around here. We've got a deadline to meet.'

It was the roughest quarrel they had had so far and it disturbed PK, especially as Johnny was quiet and preoccupied the whole day. It was unlike Johnny to brood about anything for long and if there was any misunderstanding left, PK was anxious to smooth it over with a drink or two.

As they were leaving the office he asked, 'Care to come over to my place for a drink?'

But even sitting over drinks and listening to Miles Davis could not shake Johnny out of that preoccupied mood. Eventually PK asked, 'What's eating you, Johnny?'

'It's Mouse,' he said quietly. 'I love her.'

'Oh no.'

'I'm serious, PK.'

'But Johnny. People don't fall in love these days. The movies have made that kind of thing stale. They have robbed us of our capacity to feel through feeding us with cheap sensation. Ask any man and he will tell you that he can't kiss his wife because she wants him to kiss her the way Richard Widmark kisses.'

'PK what am I going to do?'

'You're just being unrealistic. Mouse is only a woman and a rather dull, drab and colourless one at that. With your usual impetuousness you've built up an entirely false picture of her. No man in his right mind would look twice at her. The trouble with you is that you're too imaginative. You grasp at straws and turn them into threads of gold.'

'It's the inside part, PK She's got something inside her that agrees with my system.'

'What?'

'I can't explain it yet. The feeling is too fleeting but I know it's there. Somehow it's all tied up with her eyes. On the surface they're just big and dark and unfathomable but they react on me in a terrible way. They horrify me; they fascinate me; they revolt me; but why? Why? I've looked into many women's eyes; I can't ever remember feeling this way. When I talk to her and she just looks back at me with those eyes, I get a wild feeling inside. The whole thing is driving me crazy because she's so remote and unattainable. I run around this dense wall in which she has enclosed herself and there's no opening anywhere.'

'Just forget it. Think about something else. There's lots of other women in the world.'

'That's just the trouble. Four out of five nights I'm jumping into bed with a different woman. There's something about me that just makes these damn women fling themselves at me, but they mean nothing to me physically, mentally or emotionally and apart from the sex thing, I mean damn little to them too. It's messing me up. I'm just becoming a degenerate and dissipated wreck.'

'Sure and if you don't look out you'll catch a disease.'

'Be original. I said that. Please don't be facetious, PK. This is a serious matter on which I need some serious advice. You can see for yourself the way she walks around all clamped up and petrified. You can't do a thing with a woman in that state.'

'Maybe she's frigid or something.'

'You say some crazy things.'

'I may be right.'

'Because a psychologist came up with a bright idea that some women are frigid, you just lap it up. A psychologist can tell you all sorts of crap. A frigid woman just doesn't exist but there are a lot of clottish, incompetent men around. I'll admit I haven't shown any competence up to now either. I've just been living at a dizzy pace. My whole life is just one headlong rush; even if I come up against an obstacle I just want to dash it out of my way and continue the mad rush. I can't even browbeat this stupid woman into loving me. It would be like knocking against a wall. She's just made herself immune to all feeling and it just wouldn't matter one damn to her whether I loved her or not. I know that already. She forces me into taking a roundabout route. Christ! PK, I wish I didn't care one hell about the woman. These roundabout routes are not in agreement with my temperament.'

'It just calls for a bit of discipline.'

'You see. When you talk like that, I know you understand how complicated the whole thing is. I don't like those facetious remarks you've been making this evening. Discipline is just what I need.'

'God preserve me from love.'

'Now why do you say that?'

'It turns a perfectly sane human being into a raving lunatic.'

'If that's meant for me, you'd better take it back right now.'

'I was just thinking aloud.'

'Why do you waste my time with these stupid remarks?'

'I just can't believe you're serious, that's all.'

'But I am.'

'Johnny, you're really beginning to worry me. I hate to say it but Mouse is a psycho-case. I've never admitted it before but she gets me all jittery. If you get yourself mixed up with her, the consequences might be terrible.'

'I've never cared about consequences, PK, and I'm not going to start caring now. Life's too much of a challenge to me. I disagree with you about this psycho junk. Don't you see how simple the problem is? Most of us kid ourselves that someone cares about us, but she knows for a fact that no one cares one hell about her. Most kids who grow up in homes with parents just take love and affection for granted but it is the illegitimates and the unwanted ones who find out what a scarce commodity it is. Heaven alone knows why we need love, but we all need it and in some cases pretty desperately. Those who think they will never find it just clamp up and withdraw into themselves. The trouble with Mouse is that she has withdrawn so completely that it's practically impossible for me to reach her. I have to find a way to reach her. I'm not the kind of man who can love a woman in the hope that she'll one day come around to loving me. I have to do something pretty drastic about it.'

'That's just what I fear. Everything with you has to be sudden and violent and drastic.'

'Wait a minute, PK. Don't underestimate me. I'm subtle too. Damn subtle and one hell of a bastard when it comes to playing a double game. The only thing that bothers me in this instance is that the whole business has become too important to me. I'm not prepared to see myself as a possible loser. There's only one hope of reaching that clot of a woman. There's only one thing she responds to. Writing.'

'I'm really beginning to pity the kid.'

'You don't have to pity her. She survived that hell off the National Road. Why can't she survive me? I'm not half as bad as hell. I just have to convince her that I can help her with this writing business. I can too. I've spent a quarter of my life trying to figure out this writing game.'

'Johnny, you never cease to amaze me.'

'Thanks.'

'All I can say is that I hope you know what you're doing.'

'I may not know what I'm doing but I know what I want.'

7

The court closed late that Friday. As she hurried back to the office she felt a sense of shock at the casual pace of life in the street in contrast to the tense and almost unreal atmosphere of the court room. The emotion the young sailor had displayed had spread out and affected everyone, creating an unbearable tension, in a setting that demanded and nearly always got calm and impassive, blank faces. She could still hear the shocked silence as he fainted for the first time. He was a twenty-year-old Norwegian sailor on trial for contravening the Immorality Act.

A warder explained: 'Your Worship, the accused has been in the cells for two days. He has refused to eat.'

'Why?' asked the Magistrate.

An interpreter consulted briefly with the sailor and said: 'The accused says that he has not been in a prison before. It has upset him immensely. He cannot understand why he was arrested. He was only looking for a bit of fun.'

'But was the accused not aware that he was breaking a law of the country?'

'No.'

'Did he not receive instructions from his captain that it is forbidden for a White man to attempt to have, or to have, relations with a non-White woman?'

'The accused says he received no such instructions.'

'Ask the accused if he is prepared to eat. If so I shall call a temporary adjournment.'

'The accused says he cannot eat.'

The Magistrate ordered that the hearing should proceed but, in the dull drone of voices and the hot afternoon sun, the sailor again crashed to the floor in a faint.

A doctor was called.

'Your Worship, the accused appears to be of a highly-strung temperament, otherwise he is physically fit. I have given him a light sedative.'

Two warders stood on either side, holding up the sailor. His thin, small face with the sloping-away chin looked pinched and frightened. The young girl accused with him stood looking ahead impassively the way most people do when confronted with the Law. She looked like a young servant girl just recently come from the country and who had, no doubt, found it exciting to be accosted by a young man.

PK and James had already left when she reached the office. In a distracted way she noticed Johnny sitting on the edge of his desk. She sat down at her desk and frowned at her notes.

'Always the same story,' he thought. 'Can't think up a dirty lead for a dirty paper.'

'Are you looking for a lead?' he asked.

'Yes,' she said.

He read the notes quickly. 'All right,' he said. 'Here's your lead:

> *A cop peeped through a key-hole and a young man and woman found themselves in the Magistrate's Court charged with contravening the Immorality Act.*
> *'I was only looking for a bit of fun,' the man said.*
> *He was a sailor from a foreign port and said he did not know about the country's race laws . . .*

He waited impatiently as she typed out the story. When she had finished he said quietly, 'Don't go. I want to talk to you.'

She turned and stared at him with her solemn, steady gaze.

'Mouse, please avert your head a bit. I don't care to look into your eyes. They give me a horrible sensation of drowning. Thanks. Now you listen carefully to what I have to say. Whoever distributed creative gifts did not intend you to use them doing work like this. How long do you think you can go on raking around in the muck without becoming muck yourself? Not long, I'm telling you. It eats into your system and corrupts you. You can't have it both ways. Either you stay here and become muck or you pull out before it's too late. I can help you faster than you might be able to help yourself. I can help you to be the kind of writer you want to be, but there are certain conditions which go with my offer.'

'Why are you making this offer to me?'

'For the sake of destiny.'

'Destiny?'

'Mouse, don't you realize what a continent you're living in and at what a time? A new way of life is emerging in Africa and you and I, and many others, fit in somewhere. Africa may not need us but we need a country like Africa. It's just a part of this joke called Life. We need a country the way we need food and clothes. A human life is limited so it has to identify itself with a small corner of this earth. Only then is it able to shape its destiny and present its contribution. This need of a country is basic and instinctive in every living being. I don't care to admit it but historians may say we were a conquered race. Anyway, we were made to feel like the underdog. You cannot feel like the underdog and at the same time feel you belong to a country. It is the duty of the conqueror to abuse you, and treat you like an outcast and alien, and to impose false standards on you. Maybe we can help throw some of those imposed standards overboard. It is a great responsibility to be a writer at this time.'

'What are the conditions?'

'That you give me complete control to guide and direct you the way I think you should go, and that you come and live with me.'

'But I can't agree to that.'

'All right. You reject my offer. You can go now.'

'No. I mean I can't just come and live with you. You call me a clot and all that but I do know that a man and a woman don't just go and live together.'

'And why not? What's wrong with a man and a woman living together?'

'Why do you treat me like a fool, Johnny? Why do you think I'm a joke?'

'I'm not having fun. I'm dead serious.'

'But I can't come and live with you. You're a man.'

'I'm not asking you to come and live with me because you're a woman. I'm sick up to the head of women and their squirming, wriggling bodies. In fact, if I see another one, I'll pick it up and go and dump it in the sea. I'm asking you to come and live with me so that I can help you with your writing. Do you accept my offer or not?'

'I accept,' she said.

'Right. You move in now. This very day. Let's go and fetch your things.'

The house was small, square-shaped with whitewashed walls. Inside it was clean and bright with colour. There were only two rooms with a long narrow passageway down the side that led into a kitchen. Johnny led the way to the back room.

'This room is yours and the front one is mine. We'll use the kitchen to work in. I don't want you to come into my room unless it's absolutely necessary and I won't come into yours unless it's absolutely necessary. You'll have to wake me up in the morning. I have an alarm clock but I hate it, so I'd be obliged if you'll take over the job. Now. There are one or two things I want to get straightened out. I just can't have a woman around who dresses the way you do. Cut two inches off those hems and fix up the slips. Everything in here is in ship-shape order and you'll have to get yourself into shape too or else you'll never be able to think straight. I want those hems fixed up by tomorrow morning. The other item is food. I don't know what you've been shoving into yourself but it wasn't food. You've got malnutrition. In the kitchen near the stove you'll see a typed sheet. Read it. It's my idea of what food is and how important it is for the proper functioning of the human body. Can you cook?'

'No.'

'Well you'll have to learn. Cooking is just a matter of understanding how food cooks. You'll have to do a bit of cleaning up too, and buying things. You needn't worry about my room. I can fix that. Get yourself fitted in. I'm going out for a bit. I'll bring back something for supper.'

The house was warm and quiet and the noise of the slum scarcely reached into it although the street outside was filled with the screams of women and children. She happened to look up at the window and a few birds flew by with sunset on their wings. Unaccountably, a few tears trickled down but she wiped them away and unpacked her things. Dazed by the unexpectedness of events, she preferred not to think or feel. She set out her dresses and slips on the bed in preparation for turning up the hems, then she went into the kitchen. It was quite large with a red-topped table and four chairs in the centre. Against one wall was a bookcase. On a small table near the stove she found the typed sheet. She picked it up and read. It said:

> I love all the sensuous things in life. Food is one of them, so I love food. When I was a child my mother often told me I should be good so that I would go to heaven when I die.
> One day I asked her: 'What do they eat there?'
> 'Manna,' she said.
> 'What is manna?' I asked.
> She gave me a vague description but I gathered that it was something that floated around in the air like feathers. I straightaway decided that heaven was the one place where I did not want to go.
> All the things I love must be real and solid and earthy. I even want love to be as real as fresh bread and cheese. There must also be an unending supply of it.
> Our body does a lot of work for us and obligingly takes us wherever we want to go. It also works twenty-four hours, non-stop, keeping itself in order for our sake. We must take care then that we give it the proper kinds of food for its energy, for its repairs and for the way in which it fights to protect us from all kinds of ailments.

When he came back she was in her room busy with the dress hems.

'Hello Mouse,' he said gaily. 'Do you mind if I sit around here somewhere?'

He did not wait for her to reply. He stretched himself out on the floor on his back.

'I could only get two lousy packets of fish and chips but you'd better eat this apple as well. It's got something in it that's good for malnutrition. Here. Catch! I'm relieved to see that you're fixing up those hems. Your legs are quite attractive but you haven't given anyone a chance to look at them. Men like to look at women's legs. I don't know why. I really don't. I must try and figure that out some day. Did you read my hymn to food?'

'Yes,' she said, smiling.

'I didn't want to spoil it by mentioning any basic things but you just have to keep in mind things like eggs and meat and fruit and vegetables. They're all the proper foods. I wonder where all those birds are racing to? Some crazy bird-home, no doubt. The sun has set for us but they're so high up they can still reflect its light on their wings. It's damn beautiful. In one way I envy them but in another I do not. I envy them because life is simple and uncomplicated for them. I am on a par with them because inside me I feel that same high-flying freedom. I say what I like. I do what I like and I think what I like. That's what I call inner freedom. It's absolutely necessary for anyone who calls himself, or thinks himself, a writer. You won't be able to think straight in that tight bunched-up state you're in now. You've got to break off the bolts that are keeping you locked up. I said I'm going to help you with your writing. It's not difficult because you've got it all inside you. The whole principle of living and learning is dependent on what is going on in the mind. The mind is like a huge, living tapestry. Everything we see, hear, learn and experience gets fixed into this tapestry for good and, each day, more impressions are being imprinted on it. As we grow we begin to see that we can correlate those impressions into a definite pattern and so we call that our life. I think I'm wandering from the point a bit. I still had something to say about writing . . . in writing, as in every other aspect of my life, I observe no rules or style. Just the thought of having to follow a set of rules or wedging myself into a style is enough to make my hair stand on end. Style must conform to me – my every mood, whim or fantasy. I want you to feel the same way too. I want you to feel free to express yourself in an innumerable variety of styles. And another thing. Always keep in mind that the real man is alive under his skin but he is the man most often overlooked. The job of the writer is to understand that man and try to figure out all the complexities at work inside him. What more can I say except that we'll experiment as we go along. I'm going up to PK's flat for a while. You'd better get some sleep soon. You look very tired.'

8

The early morning sun awakened her and for a moment she was surprised at her strange surroundings then, as the world of sleep retreated, her feeling of surprise was supplanted by an indefinable happiness. Again she attributed it to the warmth and quiet of the small house. She pressed her head snugly into the pillow wishing to prolong the pleasant feeling for as long as possible. There was a sound of movement in the kitchen and very soon Johnny appeared with two cups of coffee.

'You needn't think I'm going to make it every morning,' he said, handing her a cup. 'Did you sleep well?'

She nodded. He stood looking down at her in an amused way. 'You're just a damn kid. I don't know what's wrong with my head.'

She looked at him with a quick, darting glance of her large eyes and there was a flicker of sharp anger in them. 'Why do you always have to insult me?'

'Oh? So you think you're something else? I'd be interested to know what.'

'I don't think I'm anything.'

'Well you'd better make a start somewhere. You can pretend you're my sister for a bit. Move over. My sister always used to sleep next to me and when I woke in the morning, she'd have her arm tight around me like this. I used to like it. It's a comforting feeling to wake up and find someone with their arm around you. Now that I come to think of it, I must have been a little in love with her too. I used to kiss her, not the way a brother should kiss a sister but the way a man kisses a woman. Like this.'

He looked at her with the amused gleam in his eyes. 'Do you think there was anything incestuous in that?'

'No,' she said.

'I think so. Society would think so too. It would condemn me as unspeakable filth for making love to my own sister. A man like that, it would say, would stop at nothing. He'd even make love to his own daughter. All I can say to society is that it's just as well I have no daughter. I'd probably make love to her too. Does that shock you?'

'No.'

'That's because you aren't aware of family relationships. I wasn't aware of them either. After my father died my mother kept on getting children from various men. There were about twelve of us altogether. She was nearly always drunk too, so we just grew up like a lot of animals. My sister was a prostitute at the age of ten. She was the eldest in the family and only did it so that we could have food to eat. She never complained, but at night she used to come and lie next to me and cry. One night she was stabbed to death. I think I would have never forgiven myself if I had withheld the kind of love she wanted from me. All that just makes me not care one hell about the laws and rules of society. They are made by men and women who know nothing about suffering. I had many reasons for asking you to come and live with me. You are about the only person I can bear to have near me now. I can't take the sham and hypocrisy and false values any longer.'

There was a loud and impatient knock on the front door. When he opened it he saw PK.

'For Christ's sake, PK, it's only six o'clock.'

'A riot's been going on the whole night. Head Office will never forgive me for this. Snap into some clothes. Tell Mouse she'd better stay at the office until six or seven and take calls. Hurry up Johnny. We've missed half the fun already.'

PK went to wait in the car. James was there too. 'I wonder if I heard right,' he said. 'Is Mouse there?'

'I don't know a thing, James,' PK said seriously.

'But I just heard . . .'

'I always believe it's safer to mind my own business.'

'I wonder.'

'What?'

'Nothing.'

'You, James, are the nicest guy I've ever met.'

'Thanks.'

'You're interested in everybody in a calm and sadistic way.'

'You may be wrong, PK. I just don't believe in wearing my heart on my sleeve.'

'I'm not complaining, James. You're a damn good reporter. That's all I'm interested in.'

Johnny came out still buttoning up his shirt and climbed in beside James. PK started the car and sped down the street.

'Hello James,' Johnny said.

'I bet you did not have time to write another short story last night.'

'Please satisfy his curiosity, Johnny. Give him all the lurid details.'

'Not this time. I'm leaving it to your imagination, James.'

'I wonder how long it's all going to last.'

'Until eternity.'

◆

The riot had broken out in a small town about fifty-six miles from Cape Town. This town had known many such riots, each riot apparently sparked off by a slight incident like a man being arrested for not being in possession of a humiliating little book. But each day, year in and year out, men and men and men were arrested for not being in possession of this humiliating little book, while the people stood by watching silently. Then, the day would come when their silent, suppressed rage would burst and they would go on a brief rampage. A garage or two would be burnt down. A shop or two looted, but, because it was like an enraged blind man striking out in his darkness, it could not balance the cost of the persecution. It merely created more shackles.

When they reached the town, the only evidence of the night's violence was those smouldering garages and the broken shop-windows. The town was quiet and the streets deserted. The people had been driven back to their small, hovel-like location surrounded by barbed wire. The Defence Force encircled them too. All that was left was for those in charge to issue the familiar statement: 'The situation is well under control.'

'We have to get inside,' PK said.

But the commander in charge refused permission. 'No one leaves or enters this location until we receive further orders.'

'You mean to say you're besieging these people?'

'I have nothing to say.'

'I recently saw a film of a German concentration camp. Somehow this strangely resembles it,' PK said.

The commander stared ahead of him and said nothing.

They walked back to the car and drove off a little way.

'We have to make a plan. Anybody got any suggestions?'

'I suggest we wait around until dark. It will be easier then to get through this army cordon. In the meantime we'd better inform the political organisations to start collecting food. This siege might be on for some time. I remember the last one lasted a week,' Johnny said.

The waiting depressed him. When they eventually managed to get into the location, the words of the people they interviewed depressed him even further: 'When something like this happens we all participate. Even the reluctant ones and the old men and women and children must participate. When there is to be retribution we must all suffer together,' they said. It was the cry of unarmed courage driven to the point of desperation.

In the car, on the way back to town he said: 'White South Africa is going to pay heavily for this one day.'

'You sound depressed, Johnny,' PK said.

'I am. I'm confused too. I support violence as a means to achieving political liberation. But I can clearly see that unarmed violence cannot pit itself against armed violence. Just where do you fit in with White South Africa, PK?'

'Johnny, I've long realized that I'm just an ordinary human being limited to an ordinary little world of my own. The forces that are manipulating my life in a certain direction are too big for me to fight against, so I just sit back and take things easy and wait for the inevitable.'

'Since the French Revolution, the underdog has been demanding equality. It's about time we were taking political and social equality for granted here, instead of having to clamour for it day after day. It completely distracts us from more useful occupations. The trouble is everybody reads Voltaire. They say: "It's all very well this equality business but we don't have to take such eccentric ideas seriously; the economic situation won't allow for it."'

'Just where do you fit in politically, Johnny?'

'Nowhere. I'm the one man who's going to fight for the cause of liberation without belonging to it.'

'You like to think you're different and extraordinary,' James said sarcastically.

'No, James. I just hate to commit myself to anyone or anything, and I hate to be a fence-sitter too.'

'You've got to be something.'

'Why?'

'Everybody sticks labels on each other these days. Someone's going to stick one on you.'

'Like what?'

'Opportunist. Fraud. Muddle-headed idealist.'

'The only reason why I like you, James, is for your fortune-telling ability. I've never known anyone like you who could predict events so accurately.'

'Are you two having a quarrel again? I can never tell.'

'Have you ever tried having a quarrel with James?'

'No.'

'Well don't try. He never sparks.'

'I'm desperately in need of a drink,' said PK. 'Anyone else in the same situation?'

'I'd rather hit it straight home.'

'Me too,' said James.

'I'm really surprised.'

'There's nothing to be surprised about, PK. James has a wife. She most probably dictates to him. Me, I've just got a bit of thinking to do. I can't afford to be dead drunk every day of the week.'

It was past midnight when he reached home. He went to her door and opened it softly. The light was out but she was not asleep. She sat up and he came and sat down beside her.

'What happened, Johnny?'

'Nothing much, except that the army has a lot of people locked up behind barbed wire. I'm glad you weren't asleep. I wanted to talk to you a bit. There was something I just could not make clear to you yesterday. I wanted you to come and live with me because I love you.'

She said nothing.

'Oh Mouse. Please listen to me. I love you with my soul but I have a body and I want to love you with my body as well.'

Silence.

'Did you hear me?'

'Yes,' she said faintly.

'You don't love me?'

'I don't know.'

'The whole thing is a bit complicated. You may not love me but I can't just let it end there. I want you. Sometimes when you want something pretty desperately that want starts dictating to you. If it tells you to wait a bit you just have to. I can wait a bit. I just want you to get it clear that I've got a fixed idea in my head that you belong to me. I seldom get these fixed ideas but when I do it's damn hard for me to unfix them. On the other hand I just can't do a thing to make you love me. If it's not there, it's just not there. I'm taking a gamble on the chance that it may grow and develop somehow. I wasn't pulling a fraud on you yesterday when I only spoke of the writing. I'm interested in that too.'

'Maybe I am a fraud.'

'Why?'

'I only live with half of myself.'

'I know. I just wish I didn't know so much about a woman's body. It prevents me from speeding things up a bit simply because it's not only your body that I want. I want all of you to be in agreement with me. You just don't know how important that is to me. It's one thing to have a woman's body but it's more important to have a woman that you love and understand and can live with, and who loves and understands and can live with you.'

'Why do you love me, Johnny?'

'Oh Mouse. I have a thousand-and-one reasons. It would take me a whole life-time to explain them all. All that has to be settled now is whether you are prepared to go on living with me in the likelihood that you may come round to loving me too. Yes or no?'

'Yes.'

'Even if you had said no, I wouldn't have accepted it. Please realize, Mouse, that this is a kind of commitment from which you can't ever be free.'

'I do.'

'It's not going to be easy. Waiting and patience are virtues I lack. I'm an impatient and passionate man. I might do just about anything to you when the mood gets me. I have a lot of good intentions but I never trust myself to carry them out. I'm a bit too fallible and human.'

'Johnny?'

'Yes?'

'I wish you did not love me.'

'That's all right. I wish I didn't too.'

'I just mean that I don't deserve it.'

'For Christ's sake, Mouse, who deserves anything? It is only arrogant and egotistic people who run around demanding worship and subservience from any unfortunate bastard who happens to cross their path. They never get what they want either. They just terrify everyone into a grotesque mimicry of worship and subservience and then they wonder why, at the first opportunity, their slaves turn on them and tear them to pieces. Life's one hell of a crazy joke. It dresses us up with insatiable yearnings and high-flying ambitions and then flings the fact of our insignificance in our faces. Half of us fall for the joke and start the mad rush after the big prizes. Some, like you and me, just can't fall for the joke. We've been hit too hard at too early an age.'

'I haven't been hit as hard as you.'

'I'm grateful for the knocks. I know my way around now. I know what I want too, and why I want it. Oh Mouse, whatever you do, don't slip into the habit of trusting me. I'm one hell of a dirty bastard with no scruples or moral principles. What is right and good for others is never right and good for me. I live without a code or a law. If you can understand that, it might help when things start busting up a bit. Goodnight for now. Don't wake me up until about midday.'

'Goodnight, Johnny.'

9

It was Sunday evening and they were walking along the beach. There was a storm far out at sea and the lightning flickered and darted in wild, jagged patterns across the dark and sombre sky.

'I once lived on this beach as a fisherman,' he said.

'You must have been many things.'

'Not really. I've never cared much for work. It was only the year I spent as a fisherman that I ever did any hard slogging work and it nearly killed me. Most of the time I'd just been sleeping around anywhere: in a cave on the mountain; in empty goods trucks; in waiting rooms – just anywhere; stealing a bit; doing odd jobs now and then. I had twenty-four hours of the day to live and learn as much as I wanted to. I used to think I hated the sea but what I really hated was hard manual labour. I hope the day arrives when all the work in the world is done by machines. Those who must have power can own a string of machines instead of keeping men enslaved to work for them. It's only unthinking clots who say they enjoy manual labour. Someone told them they had better, and that it's good for the muscles and all that crap.'

'But people work just so that they can trade and buy things. If one man owns all the machines and the power and money, how are the others going to live?'

'For Christ's sake, Mouse. I'm not an economist. I can't figure it out that way and plan things. All I'm saying is that hard labour is bad for mankind. Take it away. Give it to the machines. A man is no fool. He'll figure out another way of maintaining himself. He'll be forced to scheme his way up to bigger and better things.'

'I must say I like that. You make it sound so simple.'

'It would be if there wasn't that power-mad man waiting some-where around the corner to slip on the chains. Half of humanity is running like hell away from slavery while the other half is chasing behind, figuring out ways and means of maintaining the slave system. "Hey, come back here. It's for your own good," they shout. I should know. I've spent most of my life running from the power-mad man. It was the least I could do to avoid him. The crudest expression of the power drive is in the gangster; the most subtle and disastrous in the politician. Evil too, because in that field it affects many more people and creates more suffering. When I think of the mess we're in politically, I find myself envying James and PK. James sits happily on a fence with both eyes closed tight; PK is waiting for the inevitable. It must be peaceful to live like that. It's just fools like me who have headaches about the freedom, and rights, of the individual. I doubt if any political party can ever really guarantee that. It is a matter above the petty manipulations of politicians. It is intensely personal too. I would like to know of one man who does not consciously or subconsciously strive for the freedom to live as he wishes; move as he wishes and think as he wishes. To me the history of the world is the history of man's search for freedom.'

He looked at her attentive face turned towards him and said gently, 'I love you because you are the living symbol of freedom to me. You have struggled to survive against overwhelming odds.'

She turned her face away to hide the sudden tears that welled up.

'Why are you crying?' he asked.

'Because I cannot love.'

'Why don't you ask for help? You can't live it out on your own; it was not meant to be that way. Life on this earth is dependent on the sun, the sea, the winds and the things that grow out of the earth. I am dependent on you. The way I've lived has filled me with a feeling of insecurity; especially my relationships with women. I cannot correlate anything because most of my experiences have been meaningless and empty. My so-called love affairs have been nothing but a series of shocks and sensations. I just came to a day when I found I could not live that way any longer. Why don't you admit that you need someone too? If you are offered a leaning-post free of charge why don't you accept it? It's the most sensible thing to do.'

'But if I owe you the kind of love you want and I cannot give?'

'What do you know about love?'

'Nothing.'

'Then don't bother about it so much. Leave it alone. Let it take care of itself. The trouble with you is that you want a fortune-teller to assure you that everything is going to be okay. Life's not like that. It gets you into a perpetual mess because you have to grope your way around in the dark.'

A brief flash of lightning revealed the hopelessness and despair on her face.

'Oh Mouse. What am I going to do with you? Can't you even try a little bit? You don't have to start living all at once. Bit by bit would be quite enough.'

'I just want to be alone,' she said.

'Look Mouse. This is getting us nowhere. You see that bridge over there? I'll give you a race to it.'

She started to follow him then made a sharp turn and plunged into the sea. The waves were high and a huge, monster-like, rushing wall engulfed her.

'Mouse!' he cried in a stricken voice. For five seconds all he could see was the swirling, tumultuous waves and then the swirling monster that had engulfed her rose again and flung her out some twenty feet ahead of him. She was dazed but conscious and had started to rise by the time he reached her. In an uncontrollable fury he slapped her hard across the face.

'You crazy clot! Why did you have to do that?'

She fell back on the sand in a gesture of abject despair. He picked her up and carried her up the slope of the beach towards the road. They were caught in the head-lights of an oncoming car. The motorist stopped.

'Anything wrong?' he asked.

'Yes. This crazy woman just tried to commit suicide.'

'Why?'

'She's just got a perpetual suicide mind, that's all.'

The motorist laughed. 'They always try it again. Why didn't you just throw her back?'

'Fine idea. I will next time. Can you help? I want to get home.'

'Jump in. She your wife or something?'

'She's not my wife, thanks. She's just a lunatic.'

'I had a pal who tried it. Only thing, he made such a good job of it we had to bury him.'

He drove them to the small, white-washed house.

'Thanks,' Johnny said. 'I'm sorry your car's a bit wet.'

'Don't worry. I hope the lady won't do such a thing again.'

'Don't worry. We'll just bury her.'

He pulled her roughly inside the house and closed the door. 'I'm damned if I'm going to tolerate such stupidity. The one institution I support is the loony-bin and if you show any more signs of pulling the trick you played a while ago, I'm going to take you there. Clear off to your room and get out of those wet clothes.'

Her child-like look of guilt half-amused, half-exasperated him. Her body looked child-like too in the clinging wet clothes, as he watched her walk quietly to her room.

'Why do I have to mess around with a kid?' he thought. 'Like PK said, there are lots of women in the world.'

He went to the kitchen and made some coffee. When he took it in she was already in bed and lay with her face pressed into the pillow and her arms flung out above her head.

'Mouse,' he said gently. 'Drink this coffee. It will warm you up a bit.'

He gathered up the wet clothes on the floor, opened the window and dropped them outside.

'I'm sorry, Johnny,' she said quietly.

'There's nothing to be sorry about. You're just living the wrong way. You creep along through life in the shadows like a cat, carefully avoiding human contact. It's bound to mess you up. You lose the ability to respond to the normal human relationships of friendship and love. The only thing I'm asking you to do is to find your way back and come out of the shadows.'

'No one ever wanted me,' she said, not in self-pity but as a statement of fact.

'I know,' he said. 'I have an idea that there must be about one billion people in this world that nobody wants. One day I'm going to start a club for them all and teach them how to want each other.'

'Do you really mean that?'

'Of course.'

'I never know when you are serious or when you are just making a joke.'

'Above all the necessities of life, human beings need love and it is often the one thing most denied to them.'

'Why?'

'Because it is apart from the petty transactions of life. It is given freely and taken freely. Anything that's for free bedevils humanity. It's too accustomed to buying things.'

'Oh Johnny. I wish I could love you right now.'

'It's not something that you can wish about. Or think about. It's something you feel. Don't add love to your problem-sheet. Leave it alone. It will find its way to you somehow. Because I love you, I can wait until you are able to love me. You'd better get some sleep, you crazy, stupid, doltish, clot of a woman. God knows why I care one hell about you. Goodnight.'

'Goodnight, Johnny.'

10

PK stuck his ginger beard round the door.

'Morning slaves,' he said in his cheerful way. 'I'm giving a party on the mountain tonight. Who's not coming?'

'I don't think Mouse had better,' Johnny said.

'Why not?'

'She doesn't drink.'

James looked up with his cynical smile and was about to say something but the straight, blank look Johnny gave him made him change his mind.

'What do you say, Mouse? Coming or not?' PK asked.

She bent her head not knowing what to say. If Johnny was going? She felt she had no automatic right to go wherever he wanted to go.

'I don't know,' she said.

'Okay. You can make up your mind. Let me have those court stories you told me about yesterday. If nothing big's going on today you needn't go. Are you still working on that story, Johnny?'

'Yes. I still have one or two things to clear up.'

'Will you be coming to the party tonight?'

'Yes.'

'Fine. Mouse, I think you'd better take over those cinema notices from James. He's piled up with work. Well, get cracking, slaves.'

When PK closed the door, Johnny looked at her and said coldly, 'You might as well tell PK that you are coming to his silly party.'

James turned and looked at him.

'For Christ's sake, Johnny. Why don't you say you're just a racialist and that PK is going to give a mixed party and only invite White men and Black women and a few White prostitutes and that you hate the way Black women are suckers for White men and that you'd like to pose as the defender of the Black woman's virtue?'

'I've never seen you take your wife along to these parties.'

'She's got kids. We can't afford a baby-sitter.'

'You think of everything except the real issues, James. Those you avoid. Every man feels some sort of ownership for the woman he cares about. You don't take her because you can't bear to see her leered at by men who think she comes cheap because she's Black.'

'I'm not a racialist, thanks.'

'Of course. I'm the only racialist around here.'

He walked out slamming the door. James looked at her and grinned.

'What gives between you and Johnny?'

'I don't know what you mean.'

'I mean that you don't strike me as two people who go to bed with each other.'

She kept looking at him calmly, saying nothing.

He laughed.

'You can't fool me. People who go to bed with each other get pretty close. They even get to know what's going on in each other's mind. You two behave as though you don't know what's going on in each other's minds. Like now, for instance. He doesn't want to go to the party and you don't want to go to the party but you don't know what he wants to do and he doesn't know what you want to do. What do you have to say to that?'

'Nothing.'

He laughed again.

'You're not his kind of woman. If he really wanted you he would have taken you a long time ago. He just goes for one type. The high-society glamour doll. You look like Mahatma Ghandi.'

She looked at him with a sudden blazing anger. 'You look like a frog,' she said.

'I admit I don't know what makes Johnny tick. He lives somewhere in the realm of the genius or madman. But I do know that he's a sex-pervert and it's giving him some abnormal kick having you around.'

'Would you have the guts to tell him what you've just told me?'

'Of course. If you're not physically attractive to Johnny, you're damned attractive to me. I know your type. They're real hot mamas in bed. I've been offering myself for the past six months but you just give me the brush off. If you're scared about getting a baby there's such a thing as contraceptives, you know.'

'Can I have the cinema notices?'

'The trouble with you is that you're morbid. You just need a good rape. It's a pity I'm not the raping type.'

He threw the notices across to her and all that could be heard for a while was the clatter of their typewriters.

When she went to hand in the cinema copy to PK he said, 'Don't go. I have another job for you. Are you coming to the party?'

'Yes,' she said.

He looked at her quiet, expressionless face and laughed a bit, tried to be serious, then laughed some more.

'Johnny does not want you to come,' he said. 'Honestly, Mouse, I've never known anyone like you. Your face never gives you away. You'd be tops at poker-playing. See if you can fix up this job. Here is a list of a number of prominent White women. Ring them up and ask them if they would like to send their kids to an integrated school.'

After work PK drove them all to his flat to eat and collect the drinks and snacks for the party.

'What will you have, Mouse?' he asked. 'If you aren't accustomed to drink you'd better have some beer. We men take strong stuff.' He held out a glass of beer and she accepted it.

'What will you have, Johnny?'

'Nothing, thanks.'

PK poured drinks for himself and James and hummed a tune to show that he could not care either way. Johnny stood at the window maintaining a cold, aloof silence, as though they had all offended him in some way. PK and James talked quietly to each other and she sat quietly sipping the beer. She disliked its harsh, bitter taste and merely drank it because she was expected to. She was disturbed at the way his withdrawal and aloofness made her feel lost and alone. In an unacknowledged way she had already come to depend on him.

PK looked at his watch. 'We'd better start moving,' he said.

The mountain air was crisp and fresh and the lights of the town below blinked hazily in the sea mist that enveloped it. When the guests arrived, all friends and acquaintances of PK, they gaily set about lighting a big fire and grouped around it, talking and laughing. Somehow it unnerved her. The people were just a meaningless blur and the way they talked in high-pitched, false voices, frightened her. She moved away into the shadows and stood quietly gazing down at the town below. She felt a touch on her arm and turned and saw PK behind her with his arm around a woman.

'Hello Mouse,' he said. 'I've been looking all over for you. I want you to meet Mrs Mona Ross. She's secretary of an important women's club and is willing to give a statement on integrated schooling. Introduce yourselves. I'm busy.'

He left and she stood looking awkwardly and helplessly at the woman. Mona Ross held out a hand and gripped her firmly.

'Well, you know my name,' she said in a warm friendly voice. 'I think I heard PK call you Mouse.'

'Yes,' she said.

The woman threw back her head and laughed. 'Mouse?' she said. 'How terribly sweet. Well let's sit down, Mouse. Would you like a drink? I have one.'

She shook her head, feeling a bit out of her depth in the company of this pretty, vivacious woman with her wide smile and assertive personality. She sat down awkwardly.

'Let's get down to business,' Mona Ross said. 'I'm not at all against integrated schooling and would certainly send my children to one on condition that it's not co-educational. I'm against co-education. I think that's all I want to say on the matter. PK tells me you already have statements from other women. What did they say, if I'm not being too curious?'

'Most of them said it would help improve race relations.'

Mona Ross laughed. 'I could have guessed. It's a nice safe statement to make. What do you think?'

'I'm not interested.'

'Oh?'

'It's a foolish question to ask anyone under the circumstances.'

'How sweet. Of course, I agree with you.'

Mona Ross turned her head and looked at the men and women moving around the fire. Her gaze rested with a fascinated interest on

Johnny as he stood talking to someone near the fire. The leaping, unsteady flames dramatically highlighted the harsh, angular structures of his face.

'Who is that?' she asked eagerly.

'Johnny?'

'He works for the paper as well?'

'Yes.'

'I must get to know him. Do you think he would mind if I introduced myself?'

'I don't know.'

Mona Ross waited impatiently until he moved off alone out of the range of the firelight, then she rose and followed him. He walked about twenty yards and then finding a spot that pleased him settled down to look at the town below, which was almost completely swathed in a swirling sea mist. She came and sat down beside him.

'Cigarette?' she asked.

'Yes.'

She struck a match and in the brief flare glimpsed the amused, contemptuous smile of his mouth. It excited and challenged her.

'We don't have to be conventional in this unconventional atmosphere,' she said.

'I suppose not.'

'Oh come now. You're surely not one of those women-haters.'

'No.'

'That's fine. I love men.'

'I can see that.'

'I mean I love the provocative male types.'

He kept silent.

'You're being very difficult.'

'In what way?'

'I'm being so obvious.'

'Perhaps I don't like the provocative female types.'

'Oh but you do. I know you do. It's written all over your face.'

'I just don't mess around with White women,' he said bluntly.

'For heaven's sake. I'm just a woman.'

'Yes. When it suits you to be.'

84

'How can you be so chauvinistic.'

'You can call it that if you like. All I know is that you White women frighten me to death. You run around with façades so thick that a man just can't find a way to the real person beneath.'

'But why should you hate me because I'm White? Admittedly some Whites are monsters but we're not all like that. My club slaves itself to death fighting political issues.'

'I know all about your club. It's full of frustrated women trying to sublimate their frustration by handing out packets of sweets to the kids in the slums.'

She laughed. 'If you're accusing me of being sexually frustrated, you're right. I'm a complete mess politically as well.'

'Are you looking for sympathy?'

'Perhaps.'

'I haven't any to give away.'

'You're a beast.'

'Yes. And something worse.'

'It doesn't bother me,' she said, placing her hand on his thigh.

'It bothers me.'

'Don't you even trust my pride as a woman?'

'No.'

'I can't forgive a man who hurts my pride.'

'More than my pride would get hurt. Excuse me.'

He stood up and walked back towards the fire. It was deserted except for PK who lay on his back with a drink resting precariously on his stomach.

'Why are you all alone, PK?'

'I'm in a contemplative mood.'

'I know a woman just about twenty yards away who's in a contemplative mood too. If you walk straight down this path you're bound to meet her.'

'Thanks. Have you given up drinking?'

'No. You know I'm not that type.'

'Help yourself. The drinks are over there.'

'Where's Mouse?'

'Somewhere over there in the shadows.'

PK stood up and walked away. Johnny poured himself a drink and walked over to where he could dimly see her huddled and lonely form.

'Hiding again, huh? Creeping around in the shadows? Why don't you go and find yourself a man and hop off into the bushes with him? That's what this party is in aid of. Just listen to all those giggles and things. It's great fun, I'm telling you.'

He sat down beside her and drank quickly, leaving a little in the paper cup.

'Drink up this bit. I'm going to lie back and count the stars.'

He stretched out on his back and it was just the blue-black vault of the star-lit space above him and his isolation. A mixed feeling of anger, frustration and despair overcame him all of a sudden.

'Johnny?'

'Yes,' he said, almost harshly.

'I did not really want to come to the party.'

'Neither did I. PK always give these silly parties. It's a private joke of his. He thinks he's defeating the Immorality Act. Look Mouse. We have to get our relationship clear. I was a bit confused this morning. I would have said "No" outright but I did not know what you would say. We're not married or anything simply because I don't care one hell about that institution, but we'd better apply one or two of those rules that married people follow. You can't go wandering off on your own any longer. You have to consult me first. Is that clear?'

'Yes.'

'Why don't you come and lie down next to me? I'm not really a monster.'

'It just baffles me why you should care about me at all.' She moved down beside him.

'You can't see why I should care about you? You're damn mean. You give nothing to life and you expect it to give you nothing in return. I know all about it because I was playing that game too. I have the power to take whatever I want from life. I was determined to give nothing in return but I did not foresee the day when my bestiality would start to worry me. Oh Mouse. Just to hold you against me like this completes me in some vital way. I think I have a fear of loneliness. It's humiliating to admit.'

She laughed.

'What amuses you?'

'Your pride.'

'Sometimes you amaze me. I never expected you to come out with that one.'

'Of course. I'm a dumb clot.'

'Don't try to impress me. I can see you're getting smart, but I don't care one hell what I say to you. I could never admit to another woman that I was dependent on her. It would be something she'd use against me. I haven't as yet seen you display a capacity for feminine tricks.'

'But if I had to learn?'

'It's not something you learn. It's inborn, instinctive. Most of your instincts aren't functioning anyway.'

'I can't help feeling that I amuse you. You just want me around so that you can have a bit of fun.'

'And a bit of discipline too.'

'Discipline?'

'For Christ's sake, Mouse. I'm over-sexed. I can't run around being over-sexed all the time. It makes me feel like a pig and a psycho-case. On the one hand I'm plagued by a maddening sex drive and on the other by a monkish desire to control and sublimate it. The two can't mix. Either the one or the other must dominate. You are the only woman who has unconsciously been able to impose a restraint on me. The whole bang lot of them just fling themselves at me. It's driving me crazy. It's just my luck that I have extremely sacred ideas about women and love but no woman ever gave me the chance to express them. No religion or person taught them to me. If I've ever had any kind of religious feeling in my life it was simply achieved by lying back and looking at the stars. Those many nights I spent sleeping out in the open on the mountain like this or by the sea, I found a kind of prayer of my own. It went like this: "In the still of the night my soul in freedom soars." But, I used to be extremely lonely. I've always wanted a woman for as long as I can remember. It's just no use having a lot of love and no one to give it to.'

Laughing couples started to make their way back to the fire and the drinks. He stirred reluctantly.

'Do you think you'd be able to walk all the way home?'

'Yes,' she said.

'Let's go. I can't bear to stick around here any longer.'

◆

They had just entered the office the next morning when the phone rang.

'I can take a pretty good guess who it is. You'd better answer it,' he said.

She lifted the the phone. 'Hello.'

'Mona Ross here. I recognise your voice. Mouse?'

'Yes'

'Do me a favour. Ask PK if he'd please bring over my bathing costume. I left it in his flat. Is Johnny there?'

'Yes.'

'I'd like to speak to him.'

She handed the phone to Johnny. 'Johnny here,' he said.

'Mona Ross.'

'Yes?'

'I just had to tell you that I feel utter contempt for your attitude. How could you reject me?'

'I've given you my answer already.'

'You can't put the clock back and invent a racialism of your own.'

'This conversation is boring me.'

'Johnny, I need someone like you or else I would never have approached you.'

'Why don't you just observe the laws of your government. When the laws are changed maybe I'll take you up on your generous offer.'

'But you're abnormal. What you're saying is abnormal and sick.'

'I agree. I'm sick. I'm abnormal. Therefore, being in such a state I have to protect myself.'

'I don't understand.'

'You do. You know exactly what I mean. I'm putting the phone down.'

'Please Johnny, you don't know what you're doing to me.'

He put the phone down. 'Mouse?'

She looked at him inquiringly.

'I'm beginning to wish I had never met you.'

Her look was guarded and watchful.

'Love,' he said, 'at least my kind of love, is destructive. It is linked to my sense of purpose. Should I lose this love I would lose my purpose and I can no longer live without a purpose. I hate to say it but wherever I go, you go. If I have to jump over the precipice, I'm pulling you along with me. Maybe I have no right to do this. You are young and might prefer to believe that love is moonlight and rosy sunsets. It is not. It is brutal, violent, ugly, possessive and dictatorial. It makes no allowances for the freedom and individuality of the loved one. Lovers become one closely knit unit in thought and feeling. Should you eventually find that this love is beyond your capacity or that you cannot rise to its demands, you may leave but please make sure that you go to some place where I will never be able to find you. I can never allow you to live free and apart from me. I respect the freedom and individuality of all men and women. It is an agony to me to deprive you of yours.'

They were so wrapped up in each other that they did not hear James open the door. He stood looking at them with his patient, cynical smile.

'Some people have a talent for drama. If my wife and I ever behaved the way you two do, we'd have a nervous breakdown. Why can't you let life be simple and uncomplicated?'

'Because we're unsimple and complicated.'

'You mean you're crazy?'

'Yes.'

'The authorities will eventually catch up with you.'

'You have a great respect for authority, James.'

'I'm just being practical. Society cannot function without law and order. If I'm not being too personal, do you intend getting married or something?'

'No.'

'Why not?'

'We don't need permission to live together.'

'I give up.'

'That's the most sensible thing you've said this morning.

'It worries me though.'

'Try not to be.'

The phone rang and Johnny answered it.

'PK here. I can't make it to the office. I've got one hell-of-a hangover.'

'It's okay, PK. We'll survive without you.'

'I always get the feeling you're after my job.'

'Relax. As soon as this system is cleared up I'm going into the import and export business.'

'Mona Ross phoned. She's in a state. All I could make out of the incoherent babbling was Johnny, Johnny, Johnny. What have you done now?'

'Nothing. Don't worry. She's the kind of woman who loses her head completely and recovers it in three days' time.'

'You're a vicious bastard.'

'It's merely experience talking.'

'I don't mind if everyone takes the day off, but first see if you can collect some copy lying around and send it off. Head Office will rave if they don't receive that daily news packet.'

'Okay.'

'Bye. See you tomorrow.'

11

'Mouse, just listen to the crap I'm writing:

> *The government is using many non-Whites as a buffer*
> *between itself and the oppressed people of this country. These*
> *non-Whites are bought-over to run and man the machinery of a*
> *system which has as its end the perpetual suppression of the*
> *oppressed. This buffer group is the most powerful and lethal*
> *weapon the system is using against us. Should we destroy them*
> *first and then proceed to the real enemy? By destruction I do not*
> *necessarily mean bodily assault. We could educate them if they*
> *prove to be educable . . .*

The whole argument is wrong. I've been trying to figure out a way of making these government stooges disappear overnight and each time I come to the same conclusion. Put a few sticks of dynamite under their chairs. But, do you think I can write it down like that? Those sticks of dynamite belong to the world of action. Writing is the world of reason. You have to sound reasonable all the time if you want a scrap of whatever you write to serve a useful purpose. Sometimes I just pretend to be reasonable just so that I can get a useful idea across, but I'm not a reasonable man and when I start writing junk like this I begin to wonder if I had not better give up the writing game and plunge into a bit of action. Just how does one educate a stooge into not being a stooge? Every time I meet up with one of them I just find myself saying: "Look here. We're giving you enough rope to hang yourself." I'm not competent to write reasonably on stooges. If you think you can, you may take this piece over. Just see if you can figure out a reasonable way of demolishing them.'

'Everybody is trapped. They are trapped too.'

'They are trapped but dangerous. A whole generation of children have already been destroyed by an inferior and diluted education.'

'I can see how important your question is because many people cannot grasp the political issues involved. They are merely doing a job of work.'

'I'm not talking about dumb clots. I just pity all dumb people. I'm talking about those cunning bastards who deliberately prostitute themselves. Look, Mouse. The whole thing nauseates me. Drop it. The whole thing is beyond the bounds of reason. You cannot talk reasonably about an immoral matter.'

An easy working comradeship developed between them. They both liked writing and he was content for a time to use that medium to draw her out of that tight shell of reserve and retreat. He was in the habit of scribbling many short notes on whatever ideas occurred to him. She became accustomed to finding notes stuck under the door of her room or on her typewriter at work.

Dear Mouse,

I cannot fathom your unfeminine taste in literature. I mean, all those scientific things you read. But, it pleases me somehow. Science has liberated itself from the petty control and dictates of mankind. It has set itself up and apart, in a world which no man except the specialist in his particular field dare question and hinder. It has created a special language of its own too, which is secret and unintelligible to most men. The scientist in his laboratory is the recluse and mystic of this age. He can be a true benefactor to mankind without risk because he has created an aura of awe and respect to protect him. No man can resist the impact of his inventions. Governments fall over each other in an effort to cultivate his good favour. He is the man most free to express his purpose.

Or,

I don't care for very obscure and intellectual writers. I do not see why many interesting ideas cannot be expressed in short, simple sentences. Long, involved diatribes and obscure meanings confuse and bore the mind. The longer a sentence is, the harder it is to grasp. Study the good cartoonist closely. He conveys the essence of life in a few short strokes. He amuses too. It must be the same with a writer. His greatest fear should be that of boring himself and his readers.

Or,

Have you ever questioned the appeal that writing has for you? It can only have this appeal if it is life that excites, fascinates and moves you. Writing is the interpretation of life through words.

Or,

The funny thing about writing is that it makes you start thinking. Once you've started the process, you just can't stop. It makes you articulate too. If you write and write every day you begin to feel that your brain is like a well-preserved machine churning out things that will eventually prove to be of use to someone, somewhere.

One evening as they sat writing at the red-topped table, the front door burst open and a strident female voice called out: 'Hi Johnny!'

'I'm here at the back, Liz,' he called back.

Bouncing, jaunty footsteps sounded down the passageway. She was about to jump at him but pulled up short when she saw the other woman at the table.

'Have a seat,' he said pleasantly.

She moved her elegantly clad body into a chair at one end of the table, and stared in surprise at the woman opposite who looked back at her with a calm and impassive expression.

Liz raised a pair of smoothly painted eyebrows at Johnny questioningly.

'It's my new maid. She's illiterate. I'm teaching her to read and write,' he said.

She flashed a look at him which said: I know you, Johnny. She's not your maid.

'But she is. I even sleep in the front room and she sleeps in the back. Ask her if you're not satisfied.'

What's the game? the eyes flashed.

'I need a maid,' he said.

Are you trying to kid me?

'No,' he said.

Liz snapped open her bag, took out a packet of cigarettes and selected one with a superb and elegant gesture, and lit it. She blew out the smoke and stared across at the other woman, pleased at her advantage of smooth elegance, poise and self-confidence.

You could never be like me. Not even if you tried, the flashing eyes said haughtiiy. They fell on a piece of paper covered with small, closely-written handwriting.

'May I see what you have written? I'm terribly interested in anyone Johnny is interested in.'

She smiled as she said it but felt an intense hatred for the impassive face. It was impossible to tell if there was any emotion behind it. It was impossible to tell whether the person behind that face was alive, an enemy or a friend. With a mechanical gesture, the paper was handed to her.

Liz took the paper and read it out aloud in a firm, vibrating and well-controlled voice:

> . . . I have noticed an interesting and recurring pattern in the Immorality prosecutions that appear before court each day. The men are invariably the business-type of man; those who own warehouses, offices and so on. The women, on the other hand, are real tramps in the sense that they have an unwashed look and give off an overpowering odour of urine and woodsmoke.
>
> There are two strong deterrents which should prevent the men from cohabiting with the women.
>
> 1. The women are non-White; the men are White. It is against the laws of the country for White and non-White to cohabit.

2. *The odour and unwashed state of the women.*
    In the case of the first point, the social and business life of
these men is completely wrecked by the court proceedings,
newspaper publicity and the jail sentence.
    On the second point, it is difficult to understand how a person
who has learnt about bodily cleanliness could bear to come into
intimate contact with another to whom cleanliness is an unheard
of luxury.
    What is it that compels these men to destroy themselves?
Theirs is an act of destruction. Are they in some particular way
over-sensitive to the pressures of a sick society? How will we
ever know? Justice does not care to find out the cause. It is
merely interested in convicting a man on the evidence. The man
stands silent and helpless. Sometimes he whispers faintly: "I
have a sick wife at home and children to support. My career will
be ruined. The shock of my jail sentence may kill my wife."
    Justice merely replies: "We've established that you have
broken a Law. You must pay for it."
    The man stares blankly and mutely, struggling not to look too
closely at the doom that awaits him, silent about the cause that
led to his downfall. Could it not be that for months he had had
no normal sex relations with his wife and therefore fell victim to
a seductive whisper in the dark and lonely road. Or, is it not
simply that to the sex urge, harsh legislation and repugnant
odours are of no account?

Liz handed the paper back with a nonchalant gesture and said
patronizingly: 'It's very interesting.' Her brown eyes flashed towards
Johnny.
    'Everyone is wondering where you are these days.'
    'As you can see, I'm busy.'
    'Of course. With an illiterate maid, you should be.'
    'I haven't time for friendly chit-chat.'
    'There are one or two details we have to settle.'
    'Sure. Let's settle them now.'
    'I need a bit of privacy.'

He stood up. 'Come on,' he said.

She followed him to his room and closed the door behind her and leaned against it.

'What game are you playing now?' she demanded.

'Look here, Liz. We might have had a bit of fun together but I won't allow you to talk to me in that manner.'

'I'm in love with you.'

'You're always in love.'

'But this is the real thing. I swear it is.'

'I haven't time to waste. Why don't you pick up a nice dumb guy who will spend all his time doting on you? That's what you're really looking for. It will solve all your problems.'

'I really thought you had good taste.'

'What do you mean?'

'Her. Your new maid. I've never seen a more lousy specimen.'

He did not reply and she could make nothing out of his blank look.

She smiled. 'I know that hurt you. How did she manage to pin you down? By witchcraft, I bet.'

'You're so obvious and unsubtle that nothing you say can hurt.'

'I feel sorry for you. I know that type. Men never look at them twice and they get so desperate they do anything just to get a man.'

'You're boring me.'

'Johnny?'

'For Christ's sake. What do you want?'

'You. The way so many other women in this town want you. I don't mind being frank. We want you because we hate you. There's something in you that we can't pin down or hold on to. You never give yourself. There's always some part of you missing. Most men employ tricks and deceit to get a woman to go to bed with them. Some even have to pay to their last cent. You've had it all free. We've been doing the running, not only because of your devastating physical magnetism but because of that part of you we could never reach. I don't need second sight to know what gives between you and your maid. You've finally given her the one thing we've all wanted from you. I just have to spread the word around and she wouldn't last a day.'

'Go ahead. I'm just warning you though that I'm the one man no one should try to rub up the wrong way. I'm a master at the game of revenge.'

'You filthy swine.'

'Why don't you just clear out of here?'

'Please Johnny. I didn't mean that. I love you. Doesn't that mean anything to you?'

'No.'

'You love her. But why? What has she got that's so different from the rest of us?'

'Courage and complete sincerity.'

'You talk as though you don't belong to this earth but in reality you're just a hell of an ordinary guy chasing after rainbows that don't exist.'

'I'm chasing after them all the same.'

'Some people learn the hard way. When you've discovered that your rainbow is an illusion, I'll be around, waiting and available.'

'Thanks.'

'I'm not leaving right now. Are you going to throw me out by force?'

'No. Stick around. Make yourself comfortable. I'd better inform you though that I'm on a celibacy stunt. It's my latest craze. In fact I'm thinking of propagating a religion about it.'

'Shall I get undressed?'

'Sure. Go ahead. Do what you damn well like. The whole blasted lot of you creepy bastards are messing everything up. I'm tired. I'm sick and tired of being the big fish that has to be hooked. I'm just not biting any longer. I'm sick of bitches. I'm sick of hypocrites with sweet smiles and chains concealed behind their backs. I'm sick of this whole bloody mess called Life. It's filled with clots like you. Frustrated, unhappy, bewildered imbeciles who can't find a way to live and try to make damn sure that no one else will succeed at the game.'

'You're the smartest guy that ever lived. I wish you luck. You're going to need it too. Someday you'll meet up with a guy smarter than you and if it's the last thing I do, I'll attend the funeral. I'll even write the obituary: "This clod overestimated himself." '

She wrenched the door open and walked out banging the front door loudly.

He walked down the passage and stood between the passageway and the kitchen. She could feel the white-hot waves of anger beating out of him.

'Mouse,' he said quietly. 'Just go to your room for a bit. I can't bear to see a woman now.'

As she was about to pass him he stretched out his arms and pulled her roughly against him and kissed her with a ferocious despair. A feeling of tenderness overcame her alarm and she wound her long, thin arms about his neck in an instinctive gesture of comfort. It reached him and eased away his anger.

'Don't leave me alone like this. I get lost too. Life is meaningless and the more I try to inject it with meaning, the more meaningless it becomes,' he said.

He looked down and in her eyes saw her inarticulate struggle to reach out to him. He smiled.

'It's okay, Mouse. A short while ago I doubted if the rainbow exists. I don't any longer. I've found myself a pretty solid rainbow. Let's get back to work.'

They resumed their places at the red-topped table and he reached out for the paper she had been writing on.

'You've brought out some interesting points that I hadn't thought of,' he said.

'I find those simple statements very unsatisfactory. The problem appears to me to be very complicated and I'm almost afraid to misjudge an impression. When I look at those men in court it is as though there is a look of death on their faces, but I may be wrong. It could just be that I sit through too many Immorality cases and react personally to the humiliation of the proceedings.'

'Don't be afraid to develop your ideas, Mouse. They're yours. You can spread them out any way you like; and don't be afraid to trust your impressions either. Why, for instance, in the majority of Immorality convictions is it the business-type of man? Could it not be true that he might feel the pressures and tensions more acutely? Every sign of political unrest registers itself on the stock market. He is not fooled by increased Defence measures. He knows that at anytime anything can explode and he will be ruined overnight. He is a man staring down in fascinated horror into the abyss. One day it just gets too much for him and he leaps over the edge. That accounts for the look of death, as you say. He could not wait for it to come to him. He had to do the job himself. Some people are that way. They just snap and no one could care a damn hell why. Society would rather put a dead man in jail because it is a weak, imbecilic neurotic thing, formulating and obeying laws that verge on the border of sheer crazed insanity. I just wish I could put a stick of dynamite under it. Blow it up to hell. Look here, Mouse. That crazy woman who walked in here just now is just one out of about a hundred women I've been messing around with. I'm to blame for the whole damn mess. I had some crack in my head about women and I don't care to examine it too closely. Maybe a few more of them will come barging in and cause a hell of a riot, but you just sit tight like you did this evening. I'll have to extricate myself from it somehow. Once a man involves himself with women there's always some kind of retribution. They're the most vengeful creatures on this earth. If you start cultivating any of those feminine tricks, I'll just have to find a way of getting rid of you. I'm not going to tolerate it.'

She laughed. 'James told me the other day that you're a sex-pervert.'

'He's right. You'd better watch out for that clot. He's one hell of a fortune-teller. Sometimes he gives me the creeps with his uncanny insight. He sees everything. He hears everything and he knows everything. One day he's going to drive me to the point of desperation and I'm going to throw him out of that office window.'

'I did not believe him though. He's just like Mohammed down in the café who is always trying to sell me those pornographic postcards. He interprets life and love and sex as pornographic.'

'It can be, especially for a man. He can make a pig of himself if he has a powerful personality and many temptations come his way, but you were right not to believe James. He's found out one or two dirty stories about me and just limits me to that dirt. If I have sunk to the depths, I can also rise to the heights and that's something James will never know about me because he has not the capacity to understand the heights.'

'It hurt me though.'

'Why?'

'I have a thin skin that is easily pierced by an evil, poisoned arrow.'

'There's only one way to make yourself shock-proof. Do not be impressed by evil and do not be impressed by good. If you know evil and good the way I do, you'd really be bored. To me they hardly exist ... I'm having one hell of a bother with this bit I'm writing here. I just want to say that it is important for a writer to be uncommitted, but it's just like balancing on a tightrope. You can really slip into being an opportunist or a fence-sitter. I'm not so much against opportunism but I loathe fence-sitting. Mouse, if any crazy bastard stops you in the street one day and asks you to join his political party, don't. He's actually asking you to let him do your thinking for you. You'll find yourself tied up with a lot of dogma and cock-eyed ideas. The task of the writer is to serve humanity and not party politicians and their temporary fixations. But it's a hard path to follow. I'm having headaches over it because I'm too intensely aware of the pressures and issues and yet at the same time wish to retain my right to think for myself. I wish I did not care one hell about Africa and its destiny. It's going to mess me up. Africa is the one thing I can't afford to be uncommitted about and yet I, and every writer, should be – especially at this time of change, of patriotism and nationalism. I am most worried about the people and progress but the chaos of politics swings me from one side to the other. Politics is a religion these days. It invades every corner of life and ties you up hand and foot. I must be a fool to stand for non-commitment, yet I only wish it to be that way for the sake of my writing and my personal freedom. I want you to follow the same road.'

'I will.'

'You need not agree with everything I say. Oh Mouse. You are a very beautiful woman. It's a kind of beauty I have never seen on a human face. I can't even describe it because it is too simplified, too exalted. Sometimes when you're extremely interested in something your eyes become two pin-point lights of concentration. For Christ's sake! What are you crying about now?'

'Because . . .'

'Don't say it, Mouse. Just forget about it. Leave it alone. Clear off to bed.'

12

It was early Saturday morning. The south-east wind had brought a little rain during the night and each old slum house retained an intimate depth of dampness from the rain of the night before. The wind still blew over the town, chasing before it great gushes of chimney smoke into and beyond the clear morning air.

'How beautiful,' she whispered, captured by its alive and pulsating throb, as she hurried down the street with a basket over her arm.

A car hooted and pulled up alongside. It was the man with the penetrating black eyes who had tried to help her to find a wheel-chair.

'Hello,' he said. 'Did you find your wheel-chair?'

She laughed. 'No, but there was a lot of trouble about it.'

'Climb in and tell me all about it. Or are you in a hurry?'

'No. I've bought what I want and there's still two hours to go before I have to be at work.'

She opened the door and set the basket down carefully on the floor of the car.

'I had an idea I would meet you again,' he said.

He drove with that same swift, silent concentration out of the town and towards the sea and stopped the car at a point where they could look over the vast expanse of the sea. It was flat except for small, dancing, windswept waves.

'I come here almost every morning,' he said. 'It somehow gives me a good start. The day and my work don't oppress me so much.'

They sat silent for a while and then he said, 'There is something I have never cared to talk about to anyone, but you give me the feeling of being a sympathetic person. Sometimes it eases the burden if you can talk about it.'

She looked at him quietly and attentively.

'For as long as I can remember,' he said, 'I was interested in atomic

102

research. I read everything I could on the subject and thought nothing would prevent me from pursuing the thing I had set my mind on. Because I am Black that did not mean I could not be a scientist. My parents were rich and could have afforded to send me out of the country to study, but my mother wanted to possess me. She knew I would never come back. My father was terrified at the thought of a Black man wanting to reach out beyond his blackness, or so it was for him. To myself I was just another young man fascinated by the world of science. My parents eventually defeated me. I defeated myself too because I came to accept the idea that I was pushing ahead too fast. I might find myself an unwanted misfit wherever I went. I wanted above all to avoid that; I know I can only be successful in surroundings that will allow me to be. I did not want to spend the rest of my life fighting my blackness. It is hard to accept the fact that all a man aspires to is at the mercy of power-politics and the irrational, chaotic, wayward rule of men. But that is the way it is. Do you know what absorbs my brain, time and energy? I work in a hotel. I am manager in everything but name. All the management of the hotel is under my control, but I am not called a manager. I am called a store-keeper. I am also paid a store-keeper's wages.'

'You could still be a scientist. It's not too late.'

'Yes.'

'Much has changed in Africa.'

'I am cautious, though. If I allow my dreams to awaken, I want them to be fulfilled.'

'I understand.'

'I have become the kind of man who cannot cross a street, even when there are no cars in sight. I know my life and ambitions count as nothing to a politician, whether he be White or Black. He is not thinking about me. His energies are absorbed by the great international political intrigue. Overnight he can destroy me for the sake of a big deal. I do not want him to have so much control over my life but he has it all the same and I am helpless against his power. What applies to me applies to every single human being. We can make no plans unless we take the politicians into account. Those who do not, are trampled under by their ruthless machinery.'

'Somehow we must survive and fulfil ourselves.'

'We must. I wish I knew the secret of survival amidst chaos.'

'What is love?'

'If you have found it, you can name it. To me it is a crying, vacuous thing I cannot name. Do you love someone?'

'Someone tells me he loves me but in me there is a barrier.'

'Why?'

'His personality is too strong for me.'

'But you are not static. You can grow as strong as you like.'

'He is an impatient man and I cannot make up my mind about anything. I am afraid all the time.'

'You live with him?'

'Yes and he waits for me to love him, but I am confused about love. I don't know if I can love or what it is that makes me so afraid.'

'He must be an unusual man. Few men have the capacity for such a great love. Few men really care to understand a woman.'

'Why can't I love him?'

'But you do.'

'It is a heavy responsibility. I cannot accept it right away.'

'But you do know that you can afford to trust him completely.'

'Yes.'

'Most women are not that lucky. It's better not to try his patience too far.'

He drove her back to the small, white-washed house. On saying goodbye, he said, 'I would like to meet this unusual man. I think he and I could be friends. I will come around sometime.'

Johnny was not yet up and she made the coffee and took it in to him. His eyes were closed and she stood for a while gazing down at him with a troubled expression on her face. She touched the blankets lightly.

'Johnny. Wake up. Here's your coffee.'

He opened his eyes and laughed. 'I've been awake for the past half-hour. I had one hell of a bad dream and I've been trying to figure it out. Who were you talking to outside?'

'It was that man who tried to help me find a wheel-chair.'

He looked at her so strangely that she felt forced to explain further. 'I met him on my way home and we went for a drive to the sea.'

'I wonder what a married man would do if his wife came home and told him that she had just been for a drive to the sea with a man he doesn't even know.'

'But there was lots of time.'

'It's about getting into the car that worries me.'

'We just talked.'

'About what?'

'About the way politics interferes with people's lives.'

'And what else?'

A look of agony came over her face. 'Nothing else,' she lied. 'I just didn't think it would upset you.'

'I'm not upset, thanks. I think we're living a bit too free and easy. Oh Mouse. I'm only kidding. That wheel-chair fellow sounds quite nice. I do credit you with enough sense not to get into the car of a man you do not trust. Put that coffee down somewhere and come into bed. I want to tell you about my bad dream.'

She hesitated uncertainly.

He laughed.

'There's no need to freeze up. I promise I won't eat you up until you want to be eaten up.'

He opened a side of the blankets and she slipped off her shoes and moved in beside him. He smiled down at her.

'You're beginning to take me for granted. You think I won't do a thing to you. My words mean nothing. I can change my mind in a split second. This is a freakish situation, anyway.'

Her guarded, fearful look amused and exasperated him.

'Mouse, we're heading for a big showdown pretty soon. I'm on the waiting side but you're never coming. I can't wait forever.'

'Please let me go away.'

'You'd rather run away from a problem than face up to it and solve it. Either the problem is simple or it's complicated. If you're a bit scared of sex then it's simple. Most women are when they haven't experienced it before. You just have to tell me. I know what to do. If

it's me you want to run away from then it's complicated because I
can't let you go. I just can't.'

'I am inadequate.'

'Why don't you let me be the judge of that?'

'You're not me.'

'Damn you! Damn all your doltish inferiority complexes. I wish I
didn't care one hell about you. I wish I could tell you to get the hell
out of my life. I wish you had one green eye and one brown eye and a
squint instead. Oh Mouse. Instead of these dark and mysterious
depths that intrigue and fascinate me.'

'I don't really want to go away.'

'Then why did you say so?'

'I thought it might be a solution.'

'Oh, for Christ's sake! Where is this all going to end? We're running
around in circles. There's not another man on earth who would put
up with your insanities. You're just damn lucky you met up with me.
I'm insane too. Somewhere there's logic. It seems logical that two
insanities should be thrown together.'

'You wanted to tell me about a bad dream.'

'Never mind about that. I'm always having these crazy dreams
about death and violence. Someone's always sticking a knife into me.
It's due no doubt to this hysterical state I'm always in. I just can't
seem to relax. I can't think of a single moment in my life when I ever
could. A ferocious demon has been chasing me from the day I was
born. You've no idea how your stillness soothes me. You seem to
absorb some of this nervous energy that plagues me. You just come
as close as you can and put your arms right around me. I want to
hold you like this for a while.'

The clear, crisp morning air made their steps light and gay as they
walked to the office through the twisted streets of the slums. It
affected the Saturday morning hawkers too as they stood by their
barrows of fruit and vegetables. They called cheerfully across the
street to each other and harassed the housewives into buying their
wares.

James was in the office when they arrived.

'You are both a half-an-hour late,' he said grinning meaningfully.

'What's that to you?'

'Nothing. Except that someone just phoned to say PK is in jail. He's been arrested under the Immorality Act.'

Johnny ignored him and walked to his desk.

'For Christ's sake, Johnny. I'm not kidding. A cop phoned about ten minutes ago. He said PK asked him to tell us.'

'And so?'

'What do we do?'

'Nothing. PK hates anyone to barge too close to him, especially when he's in trouble. We'd better all just stick around. He'll come out on bail or something.'

An hour later PK walked in.

'Morning slaves,' he said as usual.

They looked at him in silence. There were a number of black bruises on his face and his lower lip was cut and swollen.

'Why is everyone so glum? There's always one hell of a racket going on in here.'

Johnny laughed. 'I knew it would happen to you sooner or later. You're just a bit too damned reckless.'

'You're always ready to think the worst. It just so happens I'm in the clear this time. Of all the crazy charges under the Immorality Act, this one beats them all. I haven't a clue as to what happened. I was pissed-drunk. I just thought I'd do a bit of bar hopping last night and ended up seeing everything double. Apparently what really happened is that a sixteen-year-old Coloured kid passed by and saw me clinging to a lamp post and on an impulse decided to give me a hand to a bench nearby. Unfortunately for her kindness, a cop van happened to patrol by just then and it was enough for them to see her with her brown arm around a so-called White man. Cops don't have to ask questions these days. They just haul you in and you have to prove your innocence somehow. The poor kid was quite cheerful about it all, but her parents made one hell of a racket in court. As I say I haven't a clue as to what happened but her bright, innocent face must have convinced the Magistrate. He dismissed the case.'

'That kid must be some foreign creature,' Johnny said quietly.

'Hardly anyone stops to help anyone these days. It's just a damn prison. How did you get all cut up like that, PK?'

'I haven't a clue about that either. My cell-mate told me this morning that I was kicked around by the cops. They thought I was a Jew.'

There was another long silence.

James turned and grinned at Johnny. 'For once the speech-maker is silent,' he said.

'You dumb clot,' Johnny said curtly. 'Look, PK why don't you let Head Office go to hell? We could all take the day off and go up to your place and listen to some jazz and have a little party.'

'I think that's a fine idea, Johnny. Come on. Let's go.'

13

It was five in the morning on Sunday and she was surprised when he woke her up as he usually slept until midday each Sunday.

'We're going to the mountain,' he said. 'I've got a new trick to the writing game that I want to teach you but I'll tell you about it when we get there. Go and fix up some food and wake me up in one hour's time.' He climbed into her bed and fell asleep again.

By six-thirty they had started off for the mountain. The town was quiet and asleep and the sun had just started to spread warm fingers of light over the roof tops. Johnny was in a happy mood and walked along at a brisk pace. She had great difficulty keeping up with him but he never once looked back to see how she was faring.

'Johnny,' she gasped, 'slow down a bit. I can't keep up with you.'

He laughed and quickened the pace. She was tired and hot and angry by the time they reached a little stream with a waterfall. He dropped onto the grass and looked at her with a dancing gleam of laughter in his eyes.

'Why did you have to walk so fast?' she demanded crossly.

'I was having a race with the sunrise. We men always have a purpose. You women follow on behind.'

'I won't do it again.'

He laughed. 'Now you're beginning to talk like a real woman.'

'But am I not a real woman?' she asked seriously.

'No. Just a shambles of unfocused atoms. Mind you. I like anything a bit unusual. Not everyone can have the privilege of being acquainted with a shambles of unfocused atoms.'

'I don't think it's something to have fun about. If I'm not a real woman to you, then I think it's a serious matter.'

'It is.'

'I shall have to make myself into a real woman.'

'You will. I consulted a fortune-teller yesterday and she said everything would be okay. I asked her: "How soon?" And she said: "Pretty soon."'

'Johnny?'

'I know what you're going to say. I wish I could love you or some such crap. Look. Just clear off from here for a bit. I want to strip and sit under that waterfall. I wouldn't like you to see my naked body. It might be bad for my morale.'

She stood up and walked away from the waterfall. The sun was beginning to edge its way up the mountain but the night clung to the shadows of the trees and the grass. Crickets, deluding themselves that the day had not arrived, chirped madly in the undergrowth. Yet she hardly heard them. She was conscious of a wild confusion inside her, not knowing quite how it had started, and struggling against it. She stumbled blindly up the narrow pathway in an aimless daze, until she heard him calling her and turned and walked back. He had not put on his shirt and the upper half of his body seemed to draw her gaze with a frightening pull. She sat down a few paces from him and forced her eyes to look at the ground.

'If you don't eat, you'll soon find that I've eaten up all the food.'

'Johnny, I have to get myself straightened out.'

'Sure.'

'You might be loving me for the wrong reasons. It would be painful to find that out later.'

'That's my worry. Not yours.'

'You just don't seem to understand. I haven't the strength to be anything. Least of all a writer.'

'Mouse. I'm warning you. You're pushing my self-control to a point beyond endurance.'

She turned her head away with a gesture of despair; he swung out his arm and slapped her hard across the face then turned his back and calmly continued eating. She touched her burning cheek caught between an urge to laugh and an urge to cry, then found that she did not want to do either. Her gaze was drawn to the magnetic, hollow curve of his back and at the same time she felt a strange sensation in her hands as though they wanted to reach out towards it. She pressed them firmly on the ground. Wondering at her silence, he turned round unexpectedly and saw a startled, guilty look on her face.

'What are you up to now? I can't turn my back on you for one minute without getting the feeling that you're up to something. Were you planning to assassinate me?'

'No.'

'Then what are you looking so guilty about?'

'I don't know,' she lied.

'Mouse. Do you know that just one of you is enough to drive ten perfectly sane people stark crazy? It's a good thing nature puts limitations on your kind. I wouldn't like to meet up with another.'

'I wish . . .'

'Please don't wish anything.'

'I wish you would listen to me. You just shout at me all the time. I can't make anything clear to you.'

'You just listen to me. If you ever talk to me again the way you did a few moments ago about not having this and not having that, I'm going to do for you what you've failed to do for yourself. I'm going to kill you. Sometimes I do favours for people if it's not going to cost me anything. I'd like to do that favour for you but I'll make damn sure it looks as though you've done the job.'

She looked back at him impassively.

'I suppose you heard me? A dead body is of no use to the world. While it's still alive you can salvage something from the wreckage. One never knows what a wreck might produce.'

He reached out suddenly and grasped her round the neck and started to throttle her. He kept up the pressure until her eyes started rolling, then let go a bit.

'Do you want to die?' he asked.

'No,' she said faintly.

'All right. Now start thinking about living and what you have to live for. I've never in my life seen so many contradictions in one human body. You're capable of rising to great heights of strength and sinking to great depths of weakness. Aren't you a puzzle, even to yourself, Mouse?'

'Sometimes I get confused.'

'You confuse yourself sometimes, but you confuse me all the time. I just can't figure you out any more. All I know is that I want you. That's about the only thing that's clear in my mind.'

'I want you too.'

'I'm sure I did not hear right. Please say that again?'

'I said I want you too.'

'It all sounds very suspicious to me. When did you get that idea in your head?'

'I think I've wanted to tell you for some time now but there was a barrier inside me. I feel I should not have said it now, too.'

'I just knew it all sounded a bit too good to be true. Mouse, why do you persist in maintaining this futile barrier? It's not necessary.'

'Your personality is too strong for me.'

'Now what do you mean by that?'

'You overwhelm me. I could get lost like that. I have to know I have the strength and independence to live too.'

'What am I going to do with you? You evolve problems faster than I can cope. In one breath you tell me you want and do not want me. I'm just sick up to the head of sleeping alone. In fact I have no intention of sleeping alone any more. As from tonight we sleep together.'

'I would prefer it if we could continue the way we have, until I feel I am ready.'

'I'm just damned if I'm going to tolerate such craziness. Oh Mouse. Your strength and independence is something I cannot interfere with. You will achieve it. Nothing can change that. It is something necessary for you. If you've set yourself a goal, it does not matter how many detours you take. You'll reach it in the end.'

'I don't think there is another man on earth like you.'

'I agree. I know I'm unique and I like to display that fact.'

'I love you.'

'Since when?'

'I don't know. It must have been for a long time.'

'You dumb clot. When will you see me the way I really am? A rapist, an alcoholic, a wild anarchist and a crazy irrationalist. When I was a kid I heard a story about a clot called Daniel who walked into a lion's den. He had a kind of faith that disarmed the ferocity of the lion. You disarm me so completely I just can't believe I've done all those terrible things to women. Things that can't even be printed on a pornographic postcard. I don't know whether to credit you with supreme cunning or incredible stupidity. You have the ability to arouse two strong, conflicting emotions in me at the same time – a fierce masculinity and a paternal protectiveness. It's only the dumb, blank child in you that makes me tolerate this crazy set-up.'

She looked at him uncertainly and he leaned towards her slowly, forcing her back flat against the ground. He placed one hand lightly on her throat.

'I'm going to kill you right now,' he said. 'I have to end this torment.'

She believed him and a look of wild fear darted into her eyes. She turned her head aside, half closing her eyes.

'Okay. Beg for mercy. Say: "Johnny, please don't kill me." I'd like to hear it. I'm a sadist too.'

Her mouth was dry but she compressed her lips tightly and then in an odd, numbed way became aware of the gentle way in which his hand caressed her throat and with that same gentleness started to move over her body. It made her feel weak and exposed and she turned her head sharply and looked at him.

'Why don't you kill me?' she asked fiercely.

'I'm only trying to kill the child in you, by degrees. I don't want the child. I want the woman.'

'Please don't torture me like this, Johnny.'

'I have to. I've never before met up with such an insane fool like you. You don't know a thing. You bore me to death. Why don't you get up and get the hell out of my life?'

'That's just what I want to do.'

'Okay. Go.'

'How can I get up when you are holding me down like this?'

'I'm not.'

'But you are. You're pressing your hand down on my chest. I can't move.'

'You damned idiot.'

'If I'm a damned idiot, you're a blasted donkey!'

'What!'

'I said you're a blasted donkey!'

'Mouse. I'm going to give you a solid beating up for swearing at me. You have to treat me with respect.'

'I do respect you, but I loathe the way you keep shouting at me and slapping me. You've done it twice already.'

'Right. Here's another one. Well? Why don't you fight back. It's no use glaring at me like that. It leaves me quite unmoved.'

'You're deliberately provoking me.'

'I just wish the problem was that simple. All I want you to do is put your arms around me so that I can get close enough to kiss you. In most countries people kiss each other. There are a few where they don't. This happens to be a kissing country. All right. You don't have to look so trapped. To some people love is just a theory from which they are emotionally detached. For those with feeling, it is a disaster in which they become hopelessly entangled. Maybe you belong to the theory group.'

He moved away. She sprang up sharply and flung her arms around his neck.

'Johnny! It's not a theory to me. I feel intensely but when I want to express it everything just goes blank.'

He maintained a stony silence.

'Johnny? Please don't be angry with me.'

She kissed him tentatively and uncertainly on the mouth. He pulled her close and said, half-amused, half-exasperated: 'To get you to do such a simple and uncomplicated thing I have to put you on the torture rack. You've been living in bits. These bits and pieces are scattered all over the place like an upturned jigsaw puzzle. I just don't know how long it's going to take to put all the pieces in place so that we finally have a sane and well-composed picture. Now listen to me. For three minutes or so try and focus all these scattered pieces. I want to kiss you but I don't want to feel that I'm kissing something that's not all there.'

He pulled her down against him and lightly kissed the two dark wings of her eyebrows.

'Here's a toast to barriers, Mouse.'

114

She was hardly conscious of her agonised cry as his hard kisses ravaged her mouth. For her it was like a dissolution of body and bones; with only a heart left; a pulsing heart awash in an ocean of rushing tornadic darkness; helpless at its own forward rushing . . .

'Mouse?'

She opened her eyes, dazed.

'You're a disgusting, primitive woman. How could you bite me like that?'

'I *bit* you?'

'Of course. Do you think I can bite my own neck? I've never met up with anything like it in my life before.'

She stared with a shocked guilt at the red mark on his throat.

'Don't worry,' he said. 'I like it that way. I'm a disgusting, primitive man. I want to know right now if these barriers are abolished. Yes or no?'

'No.'

'For Christ's sake, Mouse. We cannot have these barriers. We're so basic in what we want that there's nothing to hide or fear. Are you going to persist in this crazy notion of barriers, barriers, barriers when none really exists between us? Okay. I can see you're going to start another argument. I've had enough for now. We'll settle this business once and for all tonight.'

'Johnny?'

'Yes.'

'I love you.'

'I love you too, but I'm a bit tired of this soul business. It begins to get monotonous all by itself. All I'm telling you is that you're going to regret the way you've kept me dangling, neither here nor there. When I catch up with you I'm going to explode you. I'm going to burn you. I'm going to torture you for all those nasty, insatiable, secretive desires you've kept locked up inside you for so long. You're the most deceitful, treacherous woman it has ever been my misfortune to encounter. You built up an impenetrable wall around yourself, not through fear of men but through fear of those powerful and insatiable hungers inside you. You deceived me with a subtle treachery. You gazed at me with the innocence of a guileless child and had I been a fool, I would have taken you at face value and passed on. I don't take kindly to women who try to make fools of men. Now, you sit up and take a look at that town down there. I want to get you started on a new approach to this writing business. Look at that town the way an artist must look at it. He has to concentrate, in a compact and simplified form, its vastness, its mood, its purpose and the flow and rhythm of its life. He is lost if he concentrates on detail, the same way a writer gets lost if he starts picking at bits and pieces of life. Life is not in bits and pieces. It is a magnificent, rhythmic, pulsating symphony. I want you to feel that way about that town down there. Try sketching it until you feel you have captured its essence. Also ask yourself these questions: "What is its destiny? What is its purpose?" While you look at that town with the eye of an artist, look at it also with the eye of a writer and let there be no difference between the artist and the writer. Get started now. I'm going to sleep for a bit. I'll wake up when I've had enough.'

For the three hours that he slept, she sat sketching or quietly staring at the town, absorbed in a deep concentration. When he awoke he looked briefly at the few sketches she had done.

'I think you've grasped it quite okay. I like these long, swinging strokes you've used. Now, describe it in words in the most compact form possible.'

She wrote briefly and handed him the paper.

The town below is a strung-out, pendulous expression of power petrified into irregular concrete and steel structures. Its mass, form and plan are the result of the conscious, working harmony in the minds of many men. The interweaving patterns of its streets, roads and alleys are blood vessels and gigantic arteries conducting minute particles of life to and fro. Its purpose is to sustain human life. Its destiny is perpetual expansion.

'You are a good pupil,' he said admiringly. 'I want you to be constantly searching for new ways to express yourself. That is how your creative powers will become dynamic.'

'Johnny. I'm indebted to you.'

'You're not. I have enough of everything. I don't see what's the use of keeping it all to myself. You're welcome. I would like you to stop working for that paper.'

'No. I would not like to leave yet. I'm not yet ready to start doing writing of my own.'

'Mouse. I'm getting damn tired of this "not yet ready" song of yours.'

'I know my limitations.'

'That's about all you know. It's tough, uphill work trying to convince you of your abilities. Let's eat. I'm hungry.'

'But there isn't any more food. You ate it all up this morning.'

'I did? Well we'd better go home right now. I can't stay the whole day without food, like you. I burn up too fast. Come. We'll follow the stream until we come to a road.'

She stood up and he placed an arm around her waist drawing her close. She looked up at him and there was a warmth and intensity in her eyes.

'I am no starry-eyed, enthusiastic idealist, Mouse. I am a cripple. My love for and faith in mankind is like dry dust in the palm of my hand. You are all I have left to keep my love and faith alive. Without this love and faith in some living thing, I cannot live.'

'If I should fail you?'

'Then I will have failed too. You are a part of me.'

The small, white-washed house welcomed them with its quiet and warmth. He closed the door and stood looking down at her with a mixed expression of tenderness and amusement.

'You go into that room right now. Remove all those stupid clothes and get into bed. I want no more arguments from you. You'd better hurry up or else I'll come in there and rip them all off. Now clear off and do as I say for a change.'

He went to the kitchen, made some coffee and cut a few sandwiches.

When he entered the room she was already in bed with her face pressed into the pillow.

'You'd better sit up and eat something. You haven't eaten a thing the whole day. I don't know what you're crying about and I don't care to know either. All I'm saying is that you'd better stop it pretty quick.'

'I'm afraid,' she whispered.

'Of what?'

'Johnny. You just rush me into everything. You don't give me time to think.'

'I've given you time enough. Just shut your mouth and drink this coffee.'

'I hardly know what I am doing or why I am doing it.'

'Neither do I.'

'How can you force me into something like this?'

'You're a crazy woman. You're going to drive me crazy too. We can't go on like this. We can't. It's just not humanly possible. I'm damned if I'm going to tolerate it any longer. What's bothering you now?'

'I'm confused.'

'Well I'm not. You just come along with me and take things easy. Just don't delude yourself that you're safe. Anything can happen. Life is a treacherous quicksand with no guarantee of safety anywhere. We can only try to grab what happiness we can before we are swept off into oblivion.'

Earth and Everything

We had a heavy, unexpected shower of rain today. It lasted so long that the hard, sun-dried earth softened. Only on its fragrance of earth-wetness rising up were there traces of the smell of dry dust. The brooding rain clouds, scattered apart, had no time to gather together and flee away. They were trapped in the sunset. The flat earth and the stark, black thorn trees became a vast pool, touched and shaded by the gold-and-red streaked sky. The insects that live in the earth cracks and under the stones all tumbled out, quivering with amazement. They claimed the earth, and now pulse out a rhythm of repetitive sound, each distinct, yet blending in harmonious restraint.

All my seven faces of deceit and pretence I had put down. Only my nameless face was there because the earth was breathing, and the air was still and quiet. Then I was trapped too, like the rain clouds. I had no time to find my seven faces, for you came to me silently, and when I looked up you were there; also with your nameless face. Everything carried my decision away, left me with no choice but this mute agreement of nameless face to nameless face. Life is full of talk, and I, more than any other, talk and talk and talk. A thousand differing contradictions pour out to conceal the underground stream that is the same always, flowing, continuous. Now I am plunged in head-to-toe; amazed that my whole self flows outward into you, yet back to me again in a current of deep peace without beginning or ending.

Love is not anything I imagined it to be. Now I rapidly change my views, theories and absurd flights of fancy. I have to. All my pretences, deceit and harshness have smoothed out and fled away. A spring is released. Some part of me is carefree like a small child. My mind is clear. I am sure. Love itself is real; at least this love; as real as fresh warm bread, butter and cheese. The stormy ocean of life outside is unreal. There is no peace there; no rest in the criss-cross currents of discord and chaos. Yet we are tied to it and, for its purposes, are separate selves, each forced to move and live in separate ways. Can it be like this for us? There is the ship, tossed about on the ocean, badly damaged – yet each time it comes to the harbour which is enclosed and safe, to be renewed. So is love: enclosed and safe, re-newing, healing the scars, the over-powering need for fulfilment, completeness.

I do not hope too much. I would rather live with you tender, violent, cruel, revengeful man, overstuffed with vanity and self-importance. But if not so – to span the years alone, without you, would not shatter me. I own your nameless face. We will meet again. Always. The pattern always repeats, repeats itself. Always. Who knows when it will end – when nameless face and nameless face are one whole thing?

Africa

Not now, not ever, shall I be complete; and though the road to find
you has been desolate with loneliness, still more desolate is the road
that leads away from you. It is as though pain piles on pain in an
endless, unbroken stream, until it is the only reality. What do they do,
those who love? My world is too subjective and cannot compel me to
attempt the satiation of those insatiable desires, longings and urges
that harass and harass me. What do I do now that your face intrudes
everywhere, and you are yet essentially ashamed of me as the thing of
nothing from nowhere? Nothing I am, of no tribe or race, and because
of it full of a childish arrogance to defend myself against all of you. If
I humble myself now, it is only because the cause of my love is far
removed from the petty conflicts, divisions and strife of our time. Like
men all over, you will kill and destroy in the struggle for position and
place. The spark has caught here too. Who knows the cause behind it
all, except that at some far-off time, I hope, I hope it will be finished
and done with! See, there is no need for explanation. Each one wants
a part of you, so be what you are: Africa – the silent, cruel and fickle
lover with two sides, and two faces: bland and smiling, and twisting
and deceiving, giving all and yet giving nothing.

It is not you who needs me, but I who need you: the part of your
masculinity that is covered by layer and layer of restraint and
tradition. I feel it there, and in unreasoning female fashion; it is the
only thing that fits in with every part of me. My only terror of you is
that I do not know the way in which to crash down the barriers and
spaces that separate my depth from your depth. I have tried before,
and failed; now I am in resentful rebellion at being only a casual
body: 'They are all the same. Why, in their fear, must they overcome
us and reduce us to slavery as a thing to cater for their needs, of no
higher value than the goat and sheep and cows and the bed?'

121

Sometimes, to spite you all, we think about white men, yellow men, green men, but they are never real. It is you whom we love and you who are real to us, and through whom we seek all things.

The thing that swings you out sharp and clear above the blur of men is your complete fearlessness. It radiates as a kind of unconscious masculine generosity that cannot undignify a woman.

We all have our defences, and yours are unbreakable and unbendable. It is a tough pride and independence. We, the women, all want you; there is not an emotion or passion that you have not experienced; it is an irresistible attraction of one who can, and has, reached to the limits of human freedom. And somewhere beyond that point is the slave and the victim. Therefore, to maintain the balance between you and us, you reveal nothing. None knows whom you love, and have loved; there are a thousand memories of tenderness locked tight behind your closed, dark, and brooding face. Whether it be one night, one year, or an eternity, always it is the same: a strange richness in which much has been given and little taken away. There is rather an insane adoration, so that it is almost as though Someone, Somewhere, is keeping a tally of momentary male generosity, and in the bleakness all around is a small oasis of human warmth you helped to create.

The only reason why I always admit pain is that it seems the only constructive emotion.

If I understand the causes of my own pain it prevents me from inflicting pain on others. If I see in myself so clearly and with a shuddering horror the malice, weakness, extreme vulnerability and ignorance, I am frozen, immobile; for each demented face in the battlefield around me is my own face. Where may one flee to escape the destruction? The cause of my pain is that I am an inextricable part of the conflict. My intense desires and needs continually drive me forward. The man I least despise, yet whose face I cannot bear, is one like you, driven by an overpowering lust for power, dominance, place, position. True, we are but two sides of the same coin, and in the jigsaw riddle of life each part of you fits some exact part of me. If I could play the game all your way, there would be in it for me a terrible, precarious, and blissful kind of heaven. If I wished, there are a thousand female tricks I could use to trap you and, since my need is so great, I am unbelievably amazed that I stop to choose between you and this other road where all is silence, uncertainty and loneliness. It is clear to me that I can only breathe freely and survive among humble things. In all things around me is a great emptiness, and though I would greedily swallow you up and grasp to me your whole self, all other things would intrude. Not of my own will am I cut off from life. I would plunge in the stream hands, feet, body and soul. But here I move, on the outer edge, in petrified loneliness, and cannot even begin to comprehend the design and pattern of my isolation; cannot break it down, this invisible steel barrier. There is no way open for me to come to your side, I cannot ever ask you to come to mine. It may be that when the rage of life has ended there will be a meeting place. All I feel is cruel frustration. Tomorrow I shall flee and flee away from your maddening, deep, seductive laughter.

My Home

My home is someplace where the wind don't blow. My heart rests someplace where the wind don't blow. Strange place this, funny place this; all black, and dark, and quiet – and the wind don't blow.

Come and see my home. It's anyplace where nobody gives orders. It's any moment of surprise: two dark eyes smile wide open, astonished; then something gentle, you don't know what, caresses your cheek. It's a park in winter, and a thin old man cramped on a park bench. It's a cold blue sky and dry autumn leaves falling, falling. It's lonely, my home – and the wind don't blow.

My home is someplace far in the distance, a point on the bleak horizon. My home is the high-wire tension and dissolving warm tenderness of love; all the new tomorrows; the deep groan of laughter when you defy fools and fate and go your own way; ride high on the tide of your own thoughts, desires and, looking behind, you're far ahead, flying, flying in someplace where the wind don't blow.

Don't enter if you don't like my home. Don't look. It's a cage; timid as the eyes of a trapped beast, and quivering, defenceless. How can my home be this way: most priceless – defenceless: most valuable – valueless: most welcoming – forbidding? Tread softly – the walls breath peace. Deep, dark, black peace, and the wind don't blow.

A Personal View of the Survival of the Unfittest

A basically timid and cowardly person dare not presume to speak for others. He can only speak for himself. Though my whole life and thoughts are bent towards my country, Africa, I live a precarious existence, never knowing from one day to the next whether I shall be forced into an unwelcome and painful exile, never knowing whom it is I offend, who it is who demands absolute loyalty from me; to all, I can give nothing; to all, especially politicians and those still fighting for liberation, I ask an excuse for taking, prematurely, in advance of the chaos, dislocation and confusion around me, the privilege of a steady, normal unfoldment of my own individuality. I ask it. I have taken an advance on what I have not earned in any battlefield – human dignity. As there is a convulsion of change in Africa, so in similar fashion has there been a corresponding convulsion in my own life. This is the only fixation I allow myself. Without the liberation of Africa it would have been a super-human impossibility to release the energies, potentials and possibilities of my individuality.

At least the road is clear now. I am a part of ordinary mankind the world over, and no living man, woman or government can deprive me of it. I am neither above nor below any other man and, as I consider my life to have value and usefulness, so do I have respect and consideration for the value and usefulness of the lives of my fellow men. Though I live in Africa, I do not wish to be cut off, through hatred and fear, from any part of mankind. The sufferings of the past and present are too heavy a burden to bear. I know myself to be cut off from all tribal past and custom, not because I wish it, but because I am here, just here in the middle of nowhere, between nothing and nothing, and though it is a cause of deep anxiety, I cannot alter the fact that I am alone. Where, in an erratic, harassed, dislocated life overshadowed by uncertain political manoeuvres can one even hope to experience what it may be like to live a day-to-day existence in some ordered, normal society? Tomorrow, I may be on Mount Kenya, the next day on the river Nile, and each may reject me. Only my own face is real to me, and within this limited sphere I must create, through sheer force of will and backbone, a limitless world of human love and tenderness, for myself alone, for my own needs. Even – after observing the mockery men make of God – a religion is denied me. There is not a single church I care to enter. Though I do not know what I am doing, or where I am going, I would much rather weave the strength of my backbone into the fabric of my life. It makes me tolerant, receptive, sensitive. There is nothing pessimistic or neurotic about a backbone. It is the jauntiest, gayest thing in the world, forever driving the body, mind and soul forward in this ceaseless urge to live, live, live. It is the last thing I have left. It is simply there. I believe in it, fiercely. I may be an odd exception to believe in my backbone, but I am one with my fellow-men in the speed with which I flee from all dogma, all religions, political, social. I know it. I have an address book here with a million different organisations protesting and protesting against something. Those who would perpetuate the perse-cution and bloodshed merely delude themselves that these protests are the 'kicks', the 'craze' of the 'cause cranks' who have nothing better to do in their leisure hours. It seems to me dead serious and constructive in its long-term effects. It has never happened before in the history of the world, this continuous and unceasing protest against any form of injustice, wherever it may occur.

I read somewhere that there were once anarchists who did not believe in governments and politicians. While I share this same disbelief, it is clear that life is stuck with them for quite some eternity. They are all about in great profusion. Each one demands my absolute loyalty. There were once highway robbers, who said: 'Your money or your life!' Today, they say: 'Your politics or your life!' Am I to be flung this way and that in the mad tide? Am I never to be forgiven because I silently, stubbornly resist the coercions and propaganda of men who would control every part of my life, yet care nothing about me? They are always ready to pounce; to sweep me into oblivion if my views do not coincide with theirs. Otherwise I am unimportant.

Yet I have not the kind of courage to oppose them openly. I take the long-term fatalistic view: let the man stumble about on stage until he either moves off, or is pushed off – by someone else, not me. Even such sheer cowardliness is a terrible and sinister threat to him, so engrossed is he in a drunk ecstasy with his status of super-ego. He cannot see me; to follow him in abandoned adulation is to cut myself off from a considerable section of my fellow-men. I must formulate hatreds out of nowhere for all those who disapprove of him, or oppose him. He wants everything from us; but the day will have to come when he will be the man best fitted to dispense what we want from him: justice, equality, peace.

Personally, privately, I do not fear death, but I find myself unwilling to face a sudden and violent ending. I hold back from pitching myself into the front line to face the firing squad. Thus, I am a private person with an intense, private obsession, consumed with curiosity at the riddle of my own life. Why have I been abruptly placed, abandoned, in a crazy wilderness with an almost unbearable load of powerful inner urges that are either the test of my self-control, or the root cause of degradation, downfall and self-destruction?

Who am I? What am I? In past and present, the answer lies in Africa; in part it lies within the whole timeless, limitless, eternal universe. How can I discover the meaning and purpose of my country if I do not first discover the meaning and purpose of my own life? Today there are a thousand labels. One of them is 'crazy crank'. I do not mind being a 'crazy crank', as long as I am sure that I am a crank of my own making, as long as I resist any environmental, social, and political attempts to control and suppress my mind. 'Crankhood' and a quiet, private awareness of individual liberty are far preferable to the frantic hysteria and anxiety of keeping pace with the latest ideology of the VIPs.

Where is the Hour of the Beautiful Dancing of Birds in the Sun-wind?

Go poet by bright wide bay
Where your lone voice is the light's preserve,
And where is the hour of the beautiful
Dancing of birds in the sun-wind . . .
(Harold N. Telemaque: *The Poet's Post*)

All life flows continuously like water in the stream and I am only some of the water in the stream, never able to gauge my depth. The hours, the years, the eternities slip by too quickly, moving, changing, never the same thing. I move with this current to the ocean only to be flung back again to the stream. The cycle seems unending, repetitive.

If I were a fish in the stream, who knows, I might resist the current. I might try some way of evading, of disentangling myself from the pushing force of the current. But I am only some of the water and move forward, helplessly. Where all the water goes, I must go. I would choose any form of non-existence rather than the pain and loneliness of life. My world is small, limited, a minute tragic circle of darkness in which I grope and guess. Everything is incomprehensible to me – myself most of all. It is I who am condemned to live, yet I am singularly ill-equipped for this strange and torturing game. I play it with half a mind and half an eye, careful, watchful. There is nothing here that I may claim permanently as my own. It all crumbles. Yet my terrible greeds and fierce passions have thrust me into the wild strife. Now I am stunned by the accumulated burden of destructive acts and, instead of seeking some place to put it down and fall asleep, I pile on myself a greater burden still, and plan, and scheme, and plan, and scheme.

I think I hold the trump card. After all, I chafe and fight against being only some of the water in the stream. I would rather be the winged one above, soaring sky-high and free. Each man, when battered down and bruised, chooses his own strange way to attain that brief hour of liberation. So do I choose mine too, in wild wayward fashion. Still, I would extend that hour to two, or three, maybe four. Thus, I hold the reins in tight control, throwing out a card here, and one there, checking back on the treasures of past experience. Not one foot would I place out of step. I hide my trump card fiercely, even from myself. All is done silently, obliquely. One day, the high roaring fire that carries me upward now will crumble to ashes. I would then store up an unerasable memory, minute, second by minute, second, against the time when I am once again plunged into the grey desolation of the stream. Thus I would survive the meaninglessness, the purposelessness of loneliness. Or so I think, I hope.

I am terror-stricken all the time, of him, of them. My terror of him I can well understand, but my terror of them leaves me faint and quaking at the knees. This is an environment to beat all environments. There is more suppression, fear, and orderliness in the makeshift of life in this little village than anywhere else in the world. They cluster together and make their faces a mask of sameness, so that none may defy these inane, complacent rules. The holy order of doing the right thing is incompatible with love, which does all the wrong things. Love can never learn to choose the woman who has the highest price, or whose father possesses the greatest number of cattle. Love strikes the outcast, the beggar, the stranger, and leaves the dull, dead, complacent conformer to his safety. I know that in the end they will defeat me, that in the end they will buy him for the bride-price I do not have. I shall be the village joke, but I care less about such mockery. Love is not a game of chance. It is deliberate, calculating, staking all on one thing. Though I am the winner, they could never count the gain I've made. It is all intensely private, meaningful to myself alone. I am only terrified of an environment that cannot understand the cause of its frustration, where love is regarded as an unhealthy, obscene, unnatural phenomenon. We may liberate ourselves from alien oppressors, but when do we come alive to ourselves? A single man, a single

129

woman seeking in a desperate way to clothe the bleakness of life with the tenderness of love? Nothing can be right until a man and a woman make all things meaningful through each other.

Africa, my loved country. You have nothing to give to me. I must give you all things, and already my will and strength are stretched to breaking point. What if you remain indifferent to me? My wild restlessness seems at odds with you. I flee hither and thither, but can find no resting place. Nowhere can I stay awhile to begin some creation of my own. They say the eternal refugees give up and flee to the countries of snow and escalators, but those countries have no use for me, at least I have no use for them.

Never have I put so much concentrated effort into a temporary and impermanent achievement. Never have I kept sense, nerve, intuition keyed, taut, alert, for the slightest clue that I had put down another card in the right place in the long months of a cat and mouse game of retreat, advance, reverse. The simple truth is that I wanted him and nothing beyond that. But it was a foolhardy choice, because I cannot see how a woman can be simple and direct with a complex and difficult man like him. There is a strong streak of destructiveness in him that I had to take into account all the time. He is the spark to everything, assaulting the senses and feelings in a violent manner, creating a terrible and high nervous tension. Even now it clutches at my throat and constricts it. It seems I over-shot myself in some of the cards I put down. I had to build up an elaborate facade of experience, yet I am a woman totally lacking experience of men. All my understanding seems based on observation, because it seems that if you give your body to be burnt without love, it profits you nothing. Yet it was the only way to get him to approach me. It was the only way to provoke a reaction, because he shuts up all feeling behind a closed and impenetrable face. Now he takes it all for granted and sweeps me along from one new, shocking, dizzy height to another. All that has been, is unreal, and all that is now, is strange and new. Then there is tomorrow, which I may face alone, and the memory of the powerful passion of his body that will torment and haunt me for ever. It isn't as though I did not know it, because the only words he said that night were: 'No one must know.'

Why? Because I am the woman I am – a terrible, threatening mixture of conflict and strangeness that is unacceptable to all around me. How it works out I do not know – the public life and the private man. In one capacity there is insincerity and the ruthless thrust of ambition. In the private man there is something so beautiful that one is bowed down under the weight of a depthless love. There is some kind of pride I have. I was stung. I could have said: 'All right, get going.' But I wanted the private man, if only temporarily. So I only said: 'All right.'

But when we looked at each other we were frightened strangers, separated by a deep chasm of terror. All the months of careful approach had given no clue as to how it should be crossed. Neither could lift a foot, or a hand, to cross the five paces to the other. We quickly averted our faces. Why is love so pitiless and merciless? It seems that you have climbed a sharp and treacherous precipice towards it, but when you draw near, it waves a glittering sword in your face and you fall back, swaying for an awful, eternal minute between nothingness and nowhere. The whole body trembles uncontrollably till at any moment you expect it to shatter into a thousand fragments.

'Please hold me,' I said. 'I think I shall fall.'

This delightful formality and reserve! It seems most necessary for each to hold a part of the self back and not merge too closely. And, when a man who has restrained himself a long time eventually reaches your lips with his kiss, it is scorching hot and his heart pounds so. The broad span of his chest is like a towering mountain in the dark night. He is all quiet, flowing, dark silence, because his hands and mouth and body know all things. Life, which was an incomprehensible mystery in flat, stark dimensions expands, becomes a greater mystery still, but now all the bonds are loosened, and the darkness is a living, moving force of deep earth-harmony that has connected to itself, at last, some missing part, and now is able to travel in a smooth current back and back, deep down into itself again. In the still of the night my soul soars in freedom because the man I love is all men. Always I was a part of all life, but only now in a meaningful sense, so that the rain-wind and sun-wind of Africa beat about my face, arms, legs, and the earth-pull is strong in my body which is vividly, intensely alive.

I am in a dilemma which causes me great anxiety. I don't know what to do with this man. I have agreed in language that this is only a temporary relationship. I seldom lie, but this time I have lied, playing for time. Still, my vagabond heart and mind are no help to me. I can retain nothing, possess nothing, and I fear I shall eventually let him be and swallow the pain. A friend from America told me of a phrase they use there – 'We have psyched you' – meaning we-have-looked-you-through-and-through. Well, I have 'psyched' him. I know he loves me. I am sure of it. He would never have been able to evoke response in my difficult body if it were not so. But that's not the end of it, or the beginning. There is this terrible environment of which he is a part and he pays an awkward, but restrained homage to it. He is feudal Africa in a way I would never allow myself to be. I need this Africa too, but not for my walking and talking and thinking and eating. I believe I can live independent of any environment, but I need Africa; I need to identify myself with it for the human pride and dignity it alone can give me.

Then, there is the man himself – complex, difficult and distrustful because his personality has caused him much suffering. Women horrify him. He is a man who has great need of their bodies, yet being so intensely proud, he cannot bear to be a slave of the sex organs. There is in him a vicious pleasure in forming a relationship with a woman and then abruptly and ruthlessly destroying it. It goes on and on like this with no stopping. He is a great man, but he hardly comprehends his greatness and potential. He is a power man, but his immense and childlike humanity keeps tripping him up. The ruthlessness is diffused as generosity. How do I convince a man like that that I do not wish to trap his soul with my body? I do not wish it, but my body is there in a terrible way. I cannot put my body away somewhere. The body is a positive thing, and love without a body is negative, useless, purposeless. One cannot help but feel a pitying fear for a man who must castrate himself all the time as a sacrifice before the altar of pride. How I hate the altars and the sacrifice! How hopelessly beyond reach is the sacrificial victim! How he puts the death-touch on all who would draw near him, because to him it is right, and he is blind, blind, blind. He is leashed in by a will of steel, with heart and head so closely knit that there isn't a point at which one can begin the softening process. Always I must tread warily, lest some gesture, some caress of tenderness produce a violent reaction, a current of vibrating hatred.

I keep putting forward the environment. I want something to share the blame because I am stark-terrified at what I may be driven to do. You see, the last card I hold, face down – its name is power too. Not anything you may care to understand; being odd, personal, indrawn, it is all of my own fashioning. Still, it bears the same stamp of the thing men use against each other in the pursuit of ambition. But this is mine, made for my own use; in other words it is simply strength to live and do and achieve. I need it, though my temperament is uncomfortable with it. It seems to put the death-touch on freedom. It's a snaking thing, whipping out of control because it is only a thing to be used by me, and not to use me, my private demon about which I do not fuss. I hide its rage by an outer cloak of ease and laughter, so that I may share and live in the laughter and ease of humanity, so that I too may one day bear many children and feel my feet flat on the earth.

It is always there now, the voice of my private demon, insistent at asserting itself. I dare not heed it, as I am weakened by a bottomless and intense desire. It may leap out of control and spread the death-touch on love and freedom. After all, if all should end and I do not see my power man again, I would have only pain to swallow and loneliness to watch over. The cards of love can only be arranged up to a point. Then they must be left standing apart till love itself is able to grow, to weave and knit them together in a harmonious pattern. It means putting myself down, in a humble way, and waiting and waiting, and in the end there may be just a crumbling nothingness? How can I be sure that this is my final stopping place? I cannot know myself too well, being only a minute dot in a vast and unpredictable complex. Still the unfathomable thing is why I need this, why I need that. I cannot pretend that the restless fevers are not there. They are very real and demanding. What I object to is their destructiveness. I would seek to quieten and satisfy them in ways that are not destructive. But I seek to find my way through a man and he is wild and difficult. His own torment beats so loudly about his ears that he cannot hear me and maybe that is why I get enraged, tempted to do things that will lash back at me and leave a world of great sorrow in me, and justify the bitterness and distrust in him.

If one can examine meanness carefully, then I am a mean woman, a real Shylock measuring out the pound for a pound of flesh. From him I have gained great riches, life has spread itself out and many doors have opened. I must give my measure back. I do it all the time, putting a grain here for a grain that is given to me. As I know him, so he knows me, but he likes to tongue-lash, to wound. Once he looked at me with an off-superior smirk and burst out: 'Hypocrite!'

'Why?' I asked, startled.

'The thing I can't stand about women,' he said, intensely, 'is the way they're always counting.'

'Counting?' I said, pretending bewilderment, but I'd been hit straight on a vulnerable spot and was profoundly agitated.

He laughed harshly, sarcastically. 'What do you think I am? I outstrip everybody!'

'Oh. Do you mean that you don't want anyone near you?' I asked. Silence.

'I don't mind if you don't come back tomorrow,' I said.

◆

Just silence and an inscrutable look. Then, I had to unthink a whole chunk of my life, and it was very painful and humbling. It seems that a human relationship cannot be conducted on a pound for pound basis. If someone is generous, flinging out the surplus of his life, then someone else must be the receiver. It is humbling to be only a receiver.

I am wearied beyond belief and tormented beyond belief. Is the battle between a man and a woman never resolved? A man is like a sculptor chipping and chipping away at life. Sometimes he knocks off a whole chunk that is irreplaceable, and then has to change his vision of what is left into something he never intended. A woman is a maker of pottery, feeling life with her hands, keeping it whole, moulding it from the depths upwards. Her vision is constant, unchanging.

Why does my life weave towards a man? After I have found him and felt his hands, mouth, and body caress my whole body, I slowly begin to move along the path of understanding. He is the beginning point and a centre around which revolves a vast gulf of peace and tenderness. His body is so beautiful too, perfect, firm, and his skin is the colour of powdery black midnight. There is a terrible greed in me. I cannot let go of him.

Poor Man

'Poor Man' is adapted from the evidence given by Mr Magane of Karakobis Village, Ghanzi, before the Bechuanaland Protectorate Legislative Council's Report of the Select Committee on Racial Discrimination in Bechuanaland. The poetic expression and deep sorrow – everything – is Mr Magane's.   B.H.

I am just thinking tonight of myself and all Africans because of the sorrows we are in.

I live in a little village. I just look after my cattle. I live in a country known as the Protectorate. I don't know what kind of protection that is. I think we are being protected from being able to see. We, the black, should not see how we are being treated by the Europeans.

Our animals are being killed here. During all these years we have been asked to pay hut tax, personal tax and cow tax. We did not refuse to do that. We paid our own tax, and that for our cattle, and yet they are killed every year. There is a certain disease about: foot-and-mouth disease. It is said our cattle do not have that disease, and despite all that they are killed.

I am unable to remember the date on which I was born and I would like to compare this with the great difficulties with which the African is faced. I don't know when it started. Last year we were removed from the place where we had been living. We were sent to the South, in lion country. We were also affected by disease. I went to the Authorities to complain that we were all ill, and that we would be killed by lions. We said we had killed five lions. The Authority only said: 'Where are the skins of the lions? You should not kill a lion. It belongs to the Government. You should have brought the skins.'

I said: 'The skins don't belong to the Government. They belong to

136

us. The lions have killed our animals. The Government sent us to the lion-infested areas. Can you leave a lion to go into your cattle and not kill it?'

Authority put out its chin: 'The Government says you must not kill lions.'

I asked: 'Have you ever seen a lion?'

Authority said: 'Yes.'

Then I said: 'Did you see that it was a dreadful animal? Did you realise that nobody will leave a lion unless he is frightened?'

Authority said: 'What do you think should be done?'

I said: 'Anybody who sees a lion and is not afraid of it should shoot it.'

Authority said: 'You cannot do that. The Government forbids it.'

I said: 'Why don't you drive the lions away from our area? They should not kill our cattle. The cattle belong to us, and you have driven us into this area where there are lions.'

Authority said: 'All right, I shall report the matter to the police.'

I said: 'You cannot run away from one lion and go to another. The police are lions.'

I feel that all this is brought about by hatred, and we are hated by our Government who should be protecting us. There is a lot to be said on this matter. We have no children in schools. The children who tried to go to school were sent back. Our children should be allowed to start school and we can pay later on. It is known that we do not all have ready cash. Government just does not want to say that it does not want our children to attend school. It does not want to say that it is not interested in our children being educated.

Who would ever comfort me in all the suffering I have endured? No one can help me because I do not want to fight the Government. The law is superior to me. Where can we go if the people we are living with little our cattle? I am an old man now. We are poor, and we have been poor for a very long time. It seems that in our own land we are thieves. We are always being blamed. There is no one who loves us.

Earth Love

The sky was a brilliant red glow when he came home that evening. He could have arrived home at midday, except that to do so was unthinkable. The message must be sent on ahead, passing from mouth to mouth, scurrying along the winding African footpaths. He must then delay, dallying here and there so that on arrival home the wife would have swept the hut, shaken out the sleeping mats and prepared a special meal of good food.

For two months he had been out in the wild bush, collecting the skins of jackal. Now he would sit at home and leisurely piece together these skins into a sleeping blanket. Always in demand, a well-made sleeping blanket can fetch a good price. A jackal blanket with its thick pattern of silver and black hair is very beautiful.

For two months he had lived on wild meat of wild animals, wild berries and wild bush-watermelon.

For two months there had been only the stunning, numbing silence of the bush. Above, in the sky at evening, the brilliant flight of the red-and-white flamingo birds; on the ground, the ceaseless, heavy jog-trot of the foolish kudu; or the startled, delicate flight of buck; or the rustle, rustle of small, round, furry animals among the low thorn bushes.

'Man can never separate himself from earth and sky,' he would often think with tender amazement. 'Always they are there, flamingo birds and kudu. Wild, beautiful sunset flamingo birds and the foolish kudu.'

'What does a man love best?' he thought. 'In the bush I am only a breathing man with eyes and ears alert for the treacherous jackal. Soon, village life will close about me again. I shall drink beer and make the rounds of the village courts, and listen to the repetitious tragedies and comedies of our life. Everywhere there is some sadness.

In the village life and in the silence of the bush. Man must continually exchange one sadness for another to make his life a livable thing.'

He felt a cold rush of wind on his face. He looked up at the sky and quickened his homeward pace. There were huge streaks of rain shadows on the east and south-west horizons. It was raining there, far in the distance, and the strong south wind had rushed through it and become a cold, fresh rain-wind. The earth was so flat and broad and wide and endless that the canopy of sky overhead had to stretch with all its might to keep pace with the breadth of the earth. The sky was always brooding about this. It did not like to be outdone by the earth. At evening, it dressed itself up in a brilliant splash of red and yellow glow, leaving the earth a black, stark silhouette of thorn trees. Man had to leave off his intense preoccupation with the earth and raise his eyes to the sky. Then, it seemed, the eyes and soul of man became the wild, beautiful sunset flamingo bird flying free in the limitless space of the sky. The ache and pain and uncertainty of earth life was drowned in the peace and freedom of the sky.

'How strange,' he thought. 'One part of me is the flamingo bird. The other the foolish kudu. More often I am the foolish kudu, my feet jogging heavily along the ground. I can see neither left nor right nor behind, but only straight ahead. All things beat down on me and I dart off in one blind direction, and another. I am a slow earth man of little wit. I am the foolish kudu. How is it then that my eyes and soul drown in the flight of the wild flamingo bird? Can I be two things at once – the flamingo bird and the foolish kudu? Man cannot separate himself from earth and sky.'

There was a rumble of thunder and a flash of lightning as he entered the village. The rain-wind rushed along the village pathways and swirled about the circular mud huts. The wife was happy to see him but subdued about expressing this happiness. The children came shouting about and he spoke to them with rough, abashed male tenderness. They took the jackal skins to store away in the spare hut and fled out of the yard to continue their interrupted game.

The wife brought the basin of water so that he could wash. 'Tell me the news,' he said, taking off his tattered, soiled shirt.

'There isn't much to tell,' she said, sitting on the ground near him.

Then, all at once a lot of words poured out so that he could hardly sort out one story from the other.

'Manga's quiet wife has left him. He beat her severely, so that she had to run to the police camp in the middle of the night. He immediately took in another woman. Then it appears that he made a young girl pregnant and when this young girl called at the house, this other woman beat the young girl. Manga was roaring drunk and beat his other woman almost to death. Her cries were so terrible that the police had to be called. Manga is now in jail. Three teachers and a principal were dismissed for making school-girls pregnant. Do you know Sylvia? She works in the shop. The one of whom people say she has no food at home, but dresses like a shop-window? People are indignant about her behaviour. It is known that she has slept with many men in the village, but now it seems that her husband took up with a quiet young teacher who is now in the place. It seems that the story was whispered to Sylvia by a snake in the green grass. While the teacher was at work, Sylvia went to her house and opened her belongings. In a suitcase were many letters from Sylvia's husband. Sylvia waited there and when the young teacher returned home, Sylvia removed her high-heeled shoe and beat her about the head. She almost beat another woman's child to death. No one can forget this terrible story. Sylvia's husband has fled away, as he does not want to face the trouble. I received a report from the cattle-post that one of the bulls has his eye damaged. The young one who was not yet castrated. He got into a fight with one of the old bulls who put a horn in his eye. I thought of going to the cattle-post to attend to the matter but then I received word that you were on the way home, so instead I sent instructions about how the eye should be treated.'

She was silent a moment. The husband commented almost to himself, smiling with quiet amusement: 'We are all foolish kudus.'

'What is that?' the wife asked, puzzled. She had never heard that expression before. The husband did not reply, and the woman went about her business. She accepted him as he was, a quiet, reserved man. He could never be driven into a quarrel, and all the things in life he looked at with an interested detachment.

The wife brought him a plate of boiled ground millet over which she had put a piece of soft braised meat, spinach and pumpkin. In another plate she had two steaming fresh young mealies. While he ate, the storm clouds gathered overhead and the thunder rumbled. A small black kitten hovered near. Its eyes were grey-green and it was soft and beautiful. He tore off a long shred of meat and put it down. The kitten ate with great delicacy, then it sat down at his feet, shot one straight black leg upwards and began cleaning its tail. Also at his feet the large, fat, brown earth ants were as busy as anything. A huge team scattered over the earth, cutting down blades of grass and carrying them back to the edge of the hole. Another team gathered these deposits of grass from the edge of the hole and all the time he could see their fat round abdomens disappearing into the earth's depths. He placed his foot over the hole for a few seconds and at once caused great confusion among this well-organised community. The team outside fell back, consulting among themselves, then dropped their blades of grass and ran panic-stricken hither and hither. When he raised his foot, four large soldier ants with menacing, shiny claws waving about, slowly emerged from the hole. They surveyed the surroundings. There was nothing wrong, just maybe some foolish kudu had temporarily interfered. They consulted with the panic-stricken workers, threw about their weight a little, then walked majestically back and disappeared into the hole. The rhythm of work replaced itself, but this time with a speeded-up tempo. The rain was near.

The wife called the children home. They had eaten a while ago and now, with the first isolated drops of rain, they came tumbling and shouting and tussling into the yard, and scattered to their separate sleeping huts.

The man felt tired and content. When he entered their sleeping hut, the bed of jackal blankets was neatly prepared. There was an oil lamp, made from a Milo tin, burning in one corner. There was the thunder and rain outside. There was this hut, and his wife's quiet, warm female body which was very satisfying.